Matt smoothed the sheet of paper and read it.

You and your kind don't belong here. Get out—and your wife and daughter, too. Before it's too late. We mean business.

Matt tried to think how he could comfort Allie. "Maybe your father should, like, lay off for a while. You know. Not talk about protesting the nuclear missiles and stuff..."

"Forget it," Allie interrupted. "He'd never go back on something he believes. Even if it doesn't work, he says, at least you stood up for what you thought. Then it's part of history, even if it's just a 'little protest in a little town somewhere.' "

She looked at him fiercely, as if she dared him to disagree, when all he wanted was to be on her side. He wanted to say he'd protest with her. But the "little town somewhere" was his town, and it was his football team, too, and it seemed as though he'd waited all his life to make it. He began to feel angry, as though she had made him defend himself. Maybe it *was* better to let grownups handle this stuff, he thought...

Chugwater? Lodgepole?

Your town? Nuclear missles in 1989 — an economy gone wild today... 2011

Other Borzoi Sprinters you will enjoy

Winning by Robin F. Brancato
Uneasy Money by Robin F. Brancato
The Ruby in the Smoke by Philip Pullman
The Three Investigators Crimebusters series:
   Hot Wheels by William Arden
   Murder To Go by Megan and H. William Stine
   Rough Stuff by G. H. Stone
   Funny Business by William McCay
   An Ear for Danger by Marc Brandel

Matt's Crusade

MARGOT MAREK

*note page 148

BORZOI SPRINTERS • ALFRED A. KNOPF
New York

DR. M. JERRY WEISS, Distinguished Service Professor of Communications at Jersey City State College, is the educational consultant for Borzoi Sprinters. A past chair of the International Reading Association President's Advisory Committee on Intellectual Freedom, he travels frequently to give workshops on the use of trade books in schools.

A BORZOI SPRINTER PUBLISHED BY ALFRED A. KNOPF, INC.
Copyright © 1988 by Margot Marek
Cover art copyright © 1989 by Kam Mak
All rights reserved under International and Pan-American Copyright
Conventions. Published in the United States by Alfred A. Knopf, Inc.,
New York. Distributed by Random House, Inc., New York.
Originally published in hardcover by Four Winds Press, a division of
Macmillan Publishing Company, in May 1988. Reprinted by
arrangement with Four Winds Press.

Library of Congress Catalog Card Number: 87-36456
ISBN: 0-394-82585-3
RL: 5.0
First Borzoi Sprinter edition: August 1989

Manufactured in the United States of America
0 1 2 3 4 5 6 7 8 9

To Richard

Matt's
Crusade

Chapter One

MATT watched his father limp down to the end of the long backyard and steady himself against his metal half-crutch. "I'm ready," Mr. Tyson said. "Let me have the ball."

Matt threw the football carefully, toward his father's right shoulder. If he threw well, his father never missed. His right arm reached out to pull the ball to his chest with the ease of the player he had been in school, before a mortar shell had exploded next to him in Vietnam. "Some things you don't forget," he would say. "That's why I want you to get it right, from the beginning."

Now he cocked the football, set to throw. "Okay, Matt. Ten-yard buttonhook on five."

Matt ran, counting inside his head, turned, and saw the ball coming fast. He hugged it and grunted as it slammed into his chest. He set two fingertips to the laces, the way his dad had shown him, and threw it back. The ball was a little low, but his father leaned over on his good leg and scooped it in. "Good," he said. "Watch for a high one coming behind you on six."

Matt ran out fast, turned, and felt the ball knock back his outstretched hand.

"You have to watch it, Matt. Watch the ball right into your hands and bring it to your body. Maybe turn a little sooner, too."

Matt listened intently and tried again. He had to jump for the ball as he turned, but he caught it and held on, his feet going out from under him as he came down. He hit the ground hard, but the ball didn't get away. That was all that mattered, he thought. "Watch it, catch it, keep it," Coach Wilson always said. Well, he could do that as well as anyone. His father had taught him using those very words.

Matt had learned well and easily. He had the compact, tightly knit body of a natural athlete. When he leaped to get a ball, or even when he fell, he never looked awkward. He didn't mind getting tackled either. It didn't seem to hurt when he was playing, and if it did, it was part of the game and he hardly felt it.

He knew he was good now, but he was afraid he

was still too small to have much chance of making the middle school team. Wayne County, where he lived, was a place where football was about the most important thing you could do. Some eighth-graders even stayed back a year on purpose, to get more time to practice and grow big enough to be sure of making the varsity team in high school. Matt was starting seventh grade, beginning that long road. He knew his parents would never let him stay back a year. Besides, he wouldn't want to. School was already too easy sometimes.

I'll just have to be good, he thought. He got up, rubbing the shoulder he'd landed on.

"You okay?" his father asked. Mrs. Tyson had been angry when Matt had sprained his wrist going after a pass last year—as though his father could have prevented it.

"You have to remember that Matt's still a child," she had said. That had only made Matt mad at her.

"How'm I going to learn if he doesn't throw it hard?" Matt had asked. He didn't want his father to hold back. He needed to be stronger. He had begun to lift his father's weights when no one was around to watch.

"I'm fine," he said, handing his father the ball. "Let me go out for a long one this time."

He sprinted down the length of the yard, but the ball landed in front of him. As he stopped to pick it up, he heard band music, and he glanced around the end of the house, toward the road. The music was coming from a van with a loudspeaker on top. Behind the van, people were marching along toward the center of town, holding banners and signs and singing softly. There couldn't have been more than about fifty of them, but they took up one whole lane of the road, and there was a police car in front of the line and one in back.

Matt went down the sloping front lawn to see what the signs said. BAN THE MISSILES, he read on a sign held by a woman. KEEP WAYNE COUNTY SAFE FOR KIDS AND OTHER LIVING THINGS. NO NUKES NECESSARY, other signs said. He was just reading a banner, TEACHERS AGAINST TERROR, when his father limped up behind him.

"Oh, yes," Mr. Tyson said, "the big protest march." He sounded sarcastic. "I forgot it was today."

"You knew they were doing it?"

"It's been in the paper, and people have been talking about it." He was looking at the marchers. "Do you know any of those people, Matt? They say there's a social studies teacher—Behringer, I think. He's some kind of leader of this thing."

"Behringer? He's my teacher," Matt said, surprised. "I don't see him, though. What are they protesting about anyway?"

4

His father took a deep breath and shook his head. "There's a rumor that they want to store nuclear missiles at the army base here. Well, they *are* going to store them there, and some people don't want them to." He started back up the driveway toward the backyard.

"Wait," Matt said, coming up beside him. "Who's right?"

Mr. Tyson smiled down at Matt. "I'm glad you're still young enough to think I know for sure. To me it seems pretty simple. We're talking about defending this country if we have to, okay? And missiles are the best defense we've got, okay? So we have to have them."

Matt was quiet for a minute. If it was that simple, why were people marching? He looked at them again; now he saw Reverend James from their church and the man who owned the tree farm just outside of town.

"I know," his father said, frowning. "That still doesn't explain the marching." He walked slowly over to the porch steps, swung around on his right leg, and used his arm to brace himself as he sat down. "Look, those people marching out there think they're right, too. But I'll bet you not one of them has ever been in hand-to-hand combat. I don't want anyone ever to have to fight like that again."

Matt sat down beside him, looking, and trying

5

not to look, at his father's leg, stretched out straight in front of him. It was an artificial leg, and it didn't bend unless his father released the catch at the knee. He'd never known his father any other way, so it seemed natural, but it was still hard to think about. It gave Matt a funny feeling in his stomach when his father talked about defending the country.

He didn't do it often. Usually they'd talk about football, great games his father remembered from when he played, or crazy, dangerous adventures he'd had camping and fishing or running the river rapids in a canoe. But when Matt had been just old enough to understand, his father had told him very simply about being in the war and being hurt.

He had held Matt up to the fireplace mantel so he could touch the empty mortar shell that was just like the one that had hit him. It was long and smooth and scary. His father had said that there weren't going to be any more wars like that. That Matt didn't have to worry.

Most of the time, his father was so skillful with the artificial leg that Matt didn't think much about it at all. But he always wished that his father could run fast and tackle and show him how to do the plays they talked about. And mostly he wished that he could just be whole again. He knew his father didn't like to talk about those things because, as he said, there wasn't anything he could do about it.

"Just you learn to play well," he would say. "That'll be my fun now."

As the march moved on out of sight, Matt asked, "Dad, will you throw me another couple of high ones? I don't want Coach Wilson to think I'm too small to play."

Mr. Tyson put his arm around Matt's shoulder. "I know, Matt. When I came back to school in seventh grade, everyone but me seemed to have grown a foot, like your friend Paul."

Matt accepted the comfort in his father's words. They stood up and walked back behind the house again, Matt carrying the football.

"I just want to make it, Dad, you know? And you worked so hard teaching me."

"It's fun, Matt. You're good now. You're going to be even better."

Matt crossed his fingers and hoped it would be so. That was one thing he could do for his father.

Chapter Two

THE next Saturday morning was the final tryout for the middle school team. The boys who wanted to be on it had been working out for most of August and every day since school had begun. But Matt felt as though this was the only day that counted.

It had been only five when he first looked at the clock, and he had forced himself to go back to sleep. Now it was six, and this time he didn't even try to stay in bed. He felt the kind of crazy energy that wouldn't even let him sit down. He pulled on his jeans and a T-shirt, and drank some orange juice in the kitchen—right out of the container, since no one was looking. On the kitchen table was his father's old lucky rabbit's foot key chain and a note: "You're good enough that you don't need luck, but take this anyway. Love, Dad."

It felt good, like a pat on the back. Matt picked up the rabbit's foot and shoved it deep in his pocket.

It was still too early even to think about going over to pick up his best friend, Paul. Matt went out to the garage to work on his dirt bike. The back fender was loose, and it stuck so he couldn't back up to get out of the bike rack at school. He looked in the carefully arranged drawers under his dad's workbench and found the right bolt and nut. The job was over too soon. The kitchen clock still hadn't reached seven. He thought his mother might get up early to give him breakfast, even though it was Saturday. She liked to do that when something special was going on. But she wasn't awake yet, and he was too impatient to wait.

He threw his bag of football equipment into the basket and got on his bike to ride over to Paul's house. Maybe Paul was awake and nervous, too. Matt pedaled hard to the end of his block, then let gravity take him faster and faster down the four-block hill to where Paul's street turned off. There were no cars at all, and he sailed right down the middle. He braked just a bit for the turn. The game was to see how close to Paul's house he could get without having to pedal again. He came within three houses this time, almost a record.

Paul was sitting on the front steps, tossing pebbles at the big tree in his front yard.

"I thought you might be up," Matt said.

"Shh," Paul cautioned. "Everyone else is still sleeping. Especially my dumb sister. And she gets mad if I wake her up."

"Can we go out back and try a few plays?" Matt whispered.

Paul picked up his football from behind the porch railing and walked around the house to his backyard, with Matt close behind him. "We're okay here," he said. They took turns throwing short passes and tackling each other.

"Hey, man, you must be nervous," Matt said, as Paul lost the ball for the third time. He threw to Paul again and ran to tackle him, trying to figure out what his friend was doing wrong. "One thing is you're still looking around when you hear me coming. Try just going on straight. No, that's not it. Give me the ball." Matt caught it to his chest and waited for Paul to tackle him. As he went down, he realized that he was automatically doing the tuck and roll his father had taught him. "Like that," he said, and threw back to Paul.

"Lay off!" Paul said, walking stiffly and stretching his mouth into an idiotic grin. "I'm beginning to feel like a tackling dummy."

Matt laughed and imitated Paul's stiff walk. Like

two robots they stumped along, bumping into each other harder and harder till they fell.

Paul tried to fall the way Matt had done but instinctively put out one hand to break his fall. Finally, Matt put his arms around Paul's chest, so they'd go down together, rolling.

"Ow," Paul said as his cheek grazed the ground. "Anyway, I'm a quarterback. Remember? I'm not going to get sacked all the time."

Paul still doesn't like getting hurt, Matt thought, no matter how big he is. Even when they had been much younger, their play fights had always ended this way, if Matt happened to wrestle Paul down or managed to get his arm behind his back.

"Sorry," Matt said.

Paul looked at his watch. "Hey, it's almost eight. Let's get something to eat and go over to the field." They walked into the house as quietly as they could.

"I can't remember ever wanting anything as much as I want to make the team," Matt confessed as he watched Paul put bread into the toaster.

"I hope we don't get too nervous," Paul said. "Maybe we shouldn't eat."

"We'll get nervous, all right," Matt said. "But so will everyone else."

"Even Terry, do you think?" Terry had always been the biggest and strongest of the boys.

"I don't know," Matt answered. "Of course he'll make it. He probably weighs one-eighty already. All he has to do is stand there on the line and push. But maybe he worries, too."

"Maybe. What about us? Do you really think we have a chance?"

Matt was quiet for a minute, chewing on toast and peanut butter. He wasn't really sure what he thought. He knew Coach Wilson wanted a team that could win. He wasn't going to choose anybody just because that person wanted it most.

"Seriously," Paul said.

"I don't know." Matt looked at Paul. His black hair was still long from the summer. His mouth looked bigger, somehow, maybe because of the faint line of hair beginning to show above it. He looked older, Matt realized. He was almost a head taller than Matt now, though they had been nose-to-nose all through grade school. "You're big," Matt said. "That's important now."

"*You're* fast. Really fast," Paul said quickly. "And you don't mind getting hurt. Coach Wilson likes that."

Matt felt a little better. Paul could be awfully sarcastic sometimes, but when he liked you he really knew how to say things that made you feel terrific.

They were silent again, getting their bikes and riding the two miles to the school playing field. There were five other boys on the field already. Terry was one of them, looking huge in his shoulder pads. Like Paul, he'd grown so much over the summer he'd had to get new pants and a jersey, though many of the boys still fit into their stuff from last year's Little League. Matt did.

As he put on his pads, he looked around the locker room. He still wasn't used to all the space and the new-looking showers and benches. At middle school level, the small elementary schools around the county joined to make one larger central school. It meant bigger classes, too, and a lot more boys wanting to play football. Some of the boys he knew from his old school but hadn't seen all summer; some he didn't know at all. Some of them looked bigger than Terry. Even in his shoulder pads, Matt felt small.

"Look at that guy over there," he said, nudging Paul as they walked out to the field. "He's huge."

"Yeah," Paul said, "but he's not too sharp. He's in math and social studies with me, and he never knows anything. Maybe he was held back once or twice, and that's why he's big."

"Sometimes I wish I'd been held back. I'd have had another year to grow."

"Stop worrying," Paul said, grinning. "Anyway, you couldn't be held back if you tried." He backed away and threw his football to Matt. Matt caught it and tossed it back. Just touching the ball made him feel a little better. He could hear his father's voice in his ear. "Don't worry about what you're going to do. Just concentrate on the ball. Only the ball. Every time."

Matt concentrated as best he could. Every time he looked around, there were more boys on the field. They all looked terrific. Probably they've been practicing with their fathers all summer, too, he thought. I'll never make it.

Luckily the whistle blew before he could think any more, and the boys moved over to surround Coach Wilson, standing with his clipboard and stopwatch, looking very serious.

The rest of the morning went by in a blur. First there were warm-up exercises and a lap around the track. Coach Wilson set up simple plays and chose groups to execute them. If you were on defense the first time, you switched to offense the next. His assistant had set up the blocking sleds, and everyone had to take turns running up against them. Matt had found out in practice sessions that they were heavier than the ones they'd used in Little League and a lot harder to push. He was glad when Coach Wilson called for sprints and timed them at forty yards. Matt was still one of the fastest.

Then Coach Wilson and his assistant watched them all throw and catch passes. Matt caught two neatly, but the third was thrown too high. He leaped but could only get his fingertips on it, and it dropped. He swore at himself. It was so much harder when it wasn't Paul or his dad throwing. "Can I try that again?" he started to ask, but Coach Wilson was already watching two other players and writing things on his clipboard. Matt wished he could see what the writing said.

He tried not to think about that as Coach Wilson had them line up for the last series of plays. Dropping the pass had made him feel shaky. That's what I'm supposed to be good at, he thought. If I can't do that, I'll never make it.

When it was his turn for a play, Matt was supposed to catch a pass, and then Terry was supposed to tackle him. He counted carefully and turned just in time to have the ball sail neatly into his hands. He was just getting up speed again when the tackle came, low and hard. He fell, turning over, but the ball was safe against his chest. He stood up and tossed the ball to the coach.

"Way to hang on," Coach Wilson said. "Run a few more wind sprints and you can get away from him next time." He patted Matt's helmet and blew the whistle. "That's all, guys. Thanks for coming out. The list will go up Monday afternoon or more likely Tuesday sometime." He turned and walked off the field.

Matt almost felt cheated. "I think I blew it," he said as Paul came up to him. "I think I blew it back then when I dropped the pass."

"You can't be so sure," Paul said comfortingly. "Nobody looked that good today."

"How about you? How'd you do?" Matt asked.

"Better than usual." Paul sounded almost surprised. "I think it all went so fast I didn't have a chance to be nervous."

Matt knew he had to say "That's great," and he did, but it was hard to get the words out. He looked around and saw boys straggling away from the field, and the coach and his assistant on the sidelines, still writing on their clipboards.

"Let's get out of here," he said to Paul, pulling off his helmet and shirt as he started to walk toward the locker room.

They dressed quickly. "Let's take the shortcut around the back of the army base," Paul said. The base was right at the edge of town, and they could save almost a mile by going through the woods behind it.

Their dirt bikes bumped on the old logging trail, the wide tires stable even on the mud in the middle of the deeper ruts. The trees were far enough apart on either side so the woods didn't feel too close.

They rode silently, concentrating on avoiding the worst ruts. As they got to the top of the hill overlooking the base, they could see down into it along the clearing made for the power lines.

"Hey, what's going on?" Paul stopped. Matt looked into the woods to see what had startled him. Paul was staring intently through the heavy chain-link fence that surrounded the base. Soldiers were unloading something from a huge olive green truck. The shape of the thing was unmistakable, like a bullet grown to monster size.

"It's got to be some kind of missile," Matt said quietly, not taking his eyes from the scene below. It was being lifted off the truck by a crane. Then, as Matt and Paul watched, the crane gently lowered it, tail-end first, into what looked like a deep well made of concrete. There were three other holes nearby, but no other missiles that the boys could see. Soldiers with rifles under their arms were standing guard beside the crane, around the concrete well, and along the fence. One of them looked up in the direction of the hill where Matt and Paul stood.

"We'd better get out of here," Matt whispered. "I don't think we're supposed to be seeing this."

"Don't be stupid," Paul answered. "They must have driven that truck along the road to get here."

"Yeah, but it was all covered up, so no one could see what was inside."

"Oh, come on. What d'you think, we're going to get arrested as spies?"

Matt shook his head and stood there silently for a minute, looking down at the point of the missile, just visible at the top of the well. Then he turned and got back on his bike. Paul followed, but they didn't speak again till they were back on the main road.

Matt relaxed as the water tower at the edge of town came into sight. His hands hurt, and he realized how tightly he'd been holding the handlebars all the way out of the woods.

"That thing gives me the creeps," he said. "I wish we hadn't seen it."

"Maybe it's a fake or a decoy. You know, for practice or something," Paul said, but he obviously didn't believe it. Neither did Matt.

"It's not that I think it's going to explode or something," Matt said, trying to figure out what he did feel. "I just don't like having it around here." He thought for a moment. "Seeing it is a lot different from just talking about it. It's so big."

As they approached Matt's house, Paul said, "Why don't you ask your dad what he knows about it. Doesn't his company sell building stuff to the army? Like the cement to build that hole?"

"I can try," Matt said, "but I'm not sure he'll tell me. We were talking about missiles last week—you know, when they had that protest march. And he didn't say anything about them already having one here."

"Well, call me if he thinks that's what we saw," Paul yelled over his shoulder as Matt turned into his driveway.

Matt rode up the slope as far as he could, then slowly pushed the bike the rest of the way to the garage. He wanted a chance to think for a minute before he talked to anyone. But his father called to him from the back porch as soon as he turned toward the house. "How'd it go?"

Suddenly his mind snapped from missiles back to football. He didn't feel great about that either. He just shrugged his shoulders, and his father looked concerned.

"That bad?" he asked.

"I don't know," Matt said. "I did okay on the last play he watched. But I dropped a pass before. Mostly I'm just too small, I think."

"Maybe." His father smiled. "But size isn't everything. You're fast and you're tough."

"Coach Wilson did say 'Way to hang on' when I got tackled after I caught a pass."

"Okay." His father patted him on the back.

"Of course he also said I should do more wind sprints."

"Look, he's never going to just say you're good.

But you are. I think you're going to make it this year." His father looked down at Matt, who still felt doubtful. "And if not this year, then next year for sure." Matt knew he was trying to be comforting, but the remark only made him realize how much he wanted to make the team now.

"Anyway, come on in for lunch. I've got to go down to the shop this afternoon to work out some figures for a job we're supplying, and I can't be too late 'cause we're invited to the Clarks' for a cookout."

"Do I have to go?" Matt asked. The Clarks had two girls, one thirteen and one eleven. Matt felt funny with them now, although they had all played together when they were younger.

"Not if you don't want to," his father said. "You can ask Paul over to keep you company if you'd rather stay here."

"I'll see," Matt said.

When they got into the kitchen, Matt realized how hungry he was. He half-hugged, half-shoved his mother on the way to the refrigerator.

"Slow down," she said, laughing. "You won't starve, I promise. Wash your hands first," she added, as he started to sit down.

"How was it today?" she asked when Matt came back.

"I don't know," Matt said. "We'll all find out

Monday or Tuesday, okay?" He was tired of talking about making the team. He helped himself to a sandwich and then remembered what he'd seen in the woods.

"Dad, you know that protest march, and the missiles we were talking about?" His father nodded. "Well, they've already got one, at least one, out at the base."

"How do you know?" His father put down his sandwich and looked at Matt.

"When me and Paul were riding home on the shortcut, we saw . . ." Matt got that same shivery feeling as he pictured what they had seen. "We were up on the hill behind the army base. There were soldiers unloading this thing from a truck and soldiers all around with their guns out."

"Mmmm," his father said. "I guess they didn't expect anyone to be up there on the hill."

"We weren't spying or anything," Matt began. "We were just on the shortcut. They had this crane to unload the thing. And they put it down into a sort of cement well."

"Sounds like a missile," Mrs. Tyson said. She looked at her husband. "Is that what you've been scrambling to supply all that cement for? The newspaper said the missiles weren't supposed to be here till October."

"We saw it. Dad, honest. And I promised Paul

I'd ask you about it. Is it supposed to be a secret?"

"Hold it. I like being the man who knows everything," his father said. "But you can tell Paul to do his own asking."

Matt felt his face get hot, the way it did when he gave the wrong answer in class. He wished someone would change the subject.

His father did. "Matt," he said, "if you make the team—and I've got this feeling you will—how are we going to have our fall camping trip? You'll be playing on Saturday mornings. And it'll be too cold by Thanksgiving."

"Don't the schools get off a Monday for Columbus Day?" his wife asked. She got up to look at the school calendar posted on the front of the refrigerator. "They do."

"Perfect time," Mr. Tyson said. "Okay with you?" He looked at Matt.

"Great," Matt said, but he still felt uneasy, even though the camping trip was something he looked forward to all year. He didn't understand why his father had seemed angry when he asked about the missiles. Maybe he thought Paul was being too snoopy.

But Matt decided it couldn't be that, when his father said, "You can ask Paul to come camping, too, if you want. It might be fun to have him along."

"Maybe," Matt said. This time he looked up and smiled.

His father stood up and put his hand on Matt's shoulder. "Listen, it's not that I don't want to talk to you about missiles. I just don't want to be the one to tell the whole world about it. Look at it this way. The army probably knows what it's doing. Let them worry about missiles, and you worry about football and camping, and getting the lawn mowed this afternoon."

Matt nodded and kept on chewing. He didn't want to look at his father right then. The way Matt figured, things people told you not to worry about usually turned out to be bad.

When his dad had left, Matt cleared the table while his mother loaded the dishwasher. It was usually a good time to talk to her. "Mom, have you ever seen one of those missiles?"

"No. Well, only on TV."

"I mean for real, not a picture. Mom, they're enormous. And scary."

"Isn't that the point? Aren't they supposed to be so scary that no one will want to start a war?"

"Is that what Dad means when he says they're the best defense?"

"I think so. That and the fact that he's got a good reason to hate the kind of war we had in Vietnam."

"I guess maybe that's why he didn't want to talk about them anymore. You probably agree with him."

"I don't know, Matt. I'm really not sure. I hate the idea of having some kind of nuclear weapon right here. My friend Jan has been sending away for a lot of stuff for us to read about how bad they are. But I think Dad's probably right that we need them. And they've got to be somewhere, I suppose."

She doesn't know whether they're good or bad either, he thought, annoyed. He went out to mow the lawn. When he got hot he came in to get a drink and drifted into the den, where it was cool.

Once he was there, his eyes went immediately to the fireplace, where the mortar shell sat on the mantelpiece, looking like a bullet for a monster's gun. He took it down and held it. That's what the missile looked like, he thought. A gigantic mortar shell. But the missile had been at least as tall as a three-story house. If the mortar shell could do what it had done to his father, what could a missile like that do?

Chapter Three

MATT was dressing carefully for school. Like most of the boys, he hadn't cared much what he wore until this year. But middle school seemed different. There were lots of kids he didn't know. They came from smaller towns that didn't have schools of their own or from farms farther out of town.

The girls seemed more visible, too, most of them wearing makeup now and constantly fussing with their hair. They always seemed to be in groups of three or four, giggling as he walked by.

Matt's straight brown hair, still lighter in streaks from the sun but shorter and neater than the shagginess of the summer, was easy to comb. His gray-green eyes looked light against his tanned skin. He rolled up the sleeves of his plaid shirt and thought that his muscles did seem bigger from lifting his father's weights.

His mother stood at the door. "You look nice," she said.

He quickly put down the comb, embarrassed to be caught staring at himself. He bounded downstairs and out the door to get the daily newspaper from the mailbox. He had been thinking that it might say something about missiles being stored at the base, and what they were there for. Sitting at the kitchen table, he flipped through the paper, but there was nothing at all about the base except for a story about two soldiers who had been in a traffic accident.

He thought about asking Mr. Behringer, his social studies teacher. His dad had said he'd been leading the protest march, and Behringer seemed to know a lot about what was going on in the world. Class always began with a current events discussion, but it wasn't boring anymore, the way it had been when everyone had to bring in a newspaper story and tell about it. Mr. Behringer wanted to know what you really thought about the twenty-one-year-old drinking age or whether we should be sending more food to Africa. The only way you could give a wrong answer was if you didn't think anything at all. Then he'd tell you to go home and read the paper or talk to your parents. If they were willing to talk, Matt thought now.

He began to hurry. It might be better to ask Behringer before school, instead of in class, he decided. He finished his cereal, ran upstairs, and grabbed his books from his desk. He realized that he hadn't even looked at the grammar assignment and shrugged. It was too late to worry about it now, and he could probably fake it if he had to. He'd been listening in class.

By the time he got his bike from the garage, Paul was waiting at the end of the driveway.

"Hi," Matt said. "I'm glad you're early. I'm going to ask Mr. Behringer what he knows about the missiles before class. I have him for social studies first period."

"Your dad didn't know anything?"

"Well . . . we had talked about missiles before, but he didn't feel like talking about the one at the base. He seemed kind of mad at me for asking." Matt paused.

"What makes you think Behringer would know anything?" Paul asked. "All Mrs. Garth seems to live for is the Middle Ages. Yech."

"Behringer was in charge of that protest march last week, Dad said. Besides, don't you always have current events first?"

"Yeah, but it's always boring stuff," Paul admitted. "Anyway, *I'm* going to go see if the list is up for the team."

"He said Monday *afternoon* or Tuesday."

"Maybe he changed his mind."

"No way," Matt said. "But you better come get me if it's up." He went upstairs to his social studies classroom. He looked through the glass part of the door and saw Mr. Behringer at his desk, reading the *New York Times*. Each student got a copy of a weekly news summary, but Mr. Behringer read the *Times* every day. No wonder he seemed to know everything. Matt felt funny about going in before the rest of the kids. He didn't know this teacher very well yet, and he didn't want him to think he was trying to be special.

Mr. Behringer looked up, saw Matt at the door, and motioned for him to come in.

"Morning, Matt. What can I do for you?"

Matt hadn't thought about how to ask. Maybe it was a dumb question. "Mr. Behringer. You know the army base outside town?" Mr. Behringer nodded. "Did you know they really are putting missiles there? Has there been anything about it in your paper?"

"What makes you think that, Matt? Have your folks been talking about it?"

"We saw one," Matt said. "Me and Paul. When we took the shortcut after football practice."

"The shortcut?"

"It goes up through the woods behind the base. There's a fence you can see through. The thing was huge. They needed a big crane to lift it into a sort of well. And there were lots of soldiers guarding it."

Mr. Behringer nodded and let out his breath. "I haven't seen it myself. But it was a missile, I'm sure. There have been a few articles about the decision to use this army base for storing them." He looked up at Matt. "How do *you* feel about nuclear missiles?" he asked.

Matt knew Mr. Behringer wanted to know about his own feelings, not what his father or mother thought. "I don't like them," Matt said.

"Why? Aren't the missiles what we need to defend ourselves?"

Matt hesitated. Before he had a chance to answer, the bell rang and the classroom filled with seventh-graders.

"Hey, look at the early bird," Terry shouted at Matt.

"We'll talk more about this in class, Matt. Better sit down now," the teacher said quietly.

Mr. Behringer had rearranged the desks in a big semicircle. "We're all in this learning thing together," he had said. It had seemed weird the first day, but they were used to it now. Matt took his seat between Terry and a girl who hadn't come from their old school.

"Working for your *A* already?" Terry asked, teasing as usual.

"Oh, shut up," Matt said, loud enough to earn a frown from Mr. Behringer.

"Okay, class, let's settle down now," the teacher said. "I want to start by asking whether any of you have heard about nuclear missiles being stored at the army base here."

Matt watched silently as several hands went up.

"There he goes," Terry whispered. "My dad told me, just get the facts, but don't listen to the politics. He says Behringer's some kind of wild-eyed peace nut or something."

"What does he mean?"

"Oh, you know, against the army and guns and stuff."

Suddenly Matt realized that Mr. Behringer was looking at them angrily. "Perhaps you gentlemen would be willing to share your discussion with the rest of us?" he asked.

"I'm sorry," Matt said. It was his own question, and he was blowing it. He thought he'd take a chance and find out if everyone felt the way his father did. "I'm not sure I like the idea of having those missiles here."

Terry's hand went up and he started talking at the same time. "That's just the kind of peacenik stuff the Russians are hoping for."

"Whoa," Mr. Behringer said. "First, just let me call on you, so we can have a discussion instead of a shouting match. But what do you mean, Terry? What about the Russians?"

"They want us to give up our missiles so they can bomb us to pieces and win," Terry said.

"Do you all agree about that?" Mr. Behringer asked. He pointed at a boy named Tim who had had his hand up from the beginning. Tim had been in school with them since kindergarten. Matt had played with him then, games about space travel and computers. He was tall and strong looking, but he never could catch or hit a baseball very well, and he never even tried football. He had always been supersmart in class, not a show-off, just knowing everything.

"Why would the Russians bomb us if we're not at war?" Tim asked. "They lost twenty million people in World War II."

"I'm surprised you know that," Mr. Behringer said. Then he pointed at Mandy, the mayor's daughter, who began every sentence with, "My dad says . . ." Sure enough, she said, "My dad says if we don't have missiles, the Russians will be stronger, so they'll feel safe starting a war."

"Yeah," Terry agreed. "The only thing they respect is strength. We want peace, so we've got to be stronger."

Matt wondered whether Terry really believed that, or if he was just repeating what *his* parents said.

He wondered, too, whether all parents thought that way. Certainly his own dad did.

Tim was talking again. "But won't the Russians just build bigger missiles or bombs so they can be stronger? How will it ever stop?"

Matt caught Tim's eye and nodded. He raised his hand, wanting to agree, but Mr. Behringer spoke without calling on anyone else. "Tim's asked the important question. How does it stop?

"So far, every time the human race has invented new weapons, from gunpowder to atomic bombs, no matter how terrible they seemed to people at first, they've always been used. So if we and the Russians both have nuclear missiles, why won't they be used?"

Terry nudged Matt. "See what I mean?" he whispered. This time Matt just looked away.

The girl sitting on the other side of him started to raise her hand, then put it down again. She wasn't as pretty as Mandy, but she had a soft look that Matt liked. Her name was Allie, Matt remembered.

Mr. Behringer was talking again. "Let's adjourn this discussion, to be continued tomorrow. We'll go back to the Middle Ages now—and by the way, we'll find out about a weapon that changed the nature of war back then. Anybody know what that was?"

Nobody did.

"Do you know what people were fighting about back then, or what war was like?"

"When my dad took us to the museum in the city, we saw suits of armor," Mandy said. "Didn't they fight on horses and wear armor?"

"Yeah," Terry began, "and the new secret weapon was the can opener."

Mr. Behringer let the laughter go on for a few seconds and then went on to talk about lances and jousting and tournaments. But Matt wasn't thinking about the Middle Ages. All he could think of was the missile. Lots of people knew about it, so he didn't have to feel like a spy. On the other hand, it didn't seem to bother most people either.

Just before the bell rang, Mr. Behringer asked them to think about topics for their reports and gave them the homework assignment.

After that class, the day dragged for Matt. People checked for the team list at every break, but it never went up. He began to feel hungry midway through fourth period. He looked forward to eating lunch with Paul, as they had done every school day since kindergarten. It felt strange not having him to talk to in every class, but in middle school they tried to mix kids from the different elementary schools.

He found Paul and some of the other guys who were trying out for the team. They headed for a table at the back of the lunchroom.

Terry and Tom were already there when Matt put down his tray.

"Hey, Matt, did you hear? Coach Wilson isn't going to put up the list till tomorrow. Another sleepless night, huh?"

Matt felt uneasy, as Terry meant him to, but he just shrugged. As he listened to the other boys talking and joking, he wondered how good you had to be before you felt as sure of yourself as Terry did. He promised himself that even if it was too late to do anything about this year, he'd get at the weights again that night, even if it meant letting his father know he was doing it. Maybe he'd better try eating more, too. He looked at the leftover sandwich crusts on his plate, but they were too disgusting. Anyway, Tom had his football, and they all hurried outside to try a few plays before the next period.

Mandy and two other girls were watching, sitting on the grass at the edge of the field. It made Matt so self-conscious that he dropped the first pass Tom threw. He wished the girls would go away. He could see why they might want to watch a game, but why just hacking around? He told himself to concentrate on the ball, "only the ball," and it worked. Terry threw high and hard, and Matt stretched and caught it. Then he turned around and threw a real bullet to Tom. Terry moved to try to intercept it. He and Tom and the ball went down together as the bell rang for sixth period.

Matt had study hall. He grabbed his books from his locker and headed for the library. He made it just as the bell was ringing and slid into the first empty seat. Allie, the gentle-seeming girl who sat beside him in social studies class, was next to him again.

He tried to think of a question to ask her, just to see what her voice sounded like, but everything he thought of seemed silly. He turned just a little to look at her, then quickly turned back before she could notice. Finally, he opened his math book and started on the first homework problem. It was mostly just review so far, so he was already halfway through the seventh one when Allie spoke to him.

"Can you show me how you did the fifth problem?" she asked. "I'm in your math class."

"Social studies, too," he said. "Yeah, sure. When you do something on one side of the equals sign, you have to do the same on the other side. You get rid of the extra stuff that way, like subtracting five from each side for this one."

"Like this?" she asked, writing out the problem.

Matt leaned over to look at her paper. Her hair brushed against his cheek, feeling as smooth as silk. He wished he had the nerve to reach out and touch it.

"Well," she asked, "is it right?"

"Perfect."

"Thanks," she said, and started to copy the next problem.

"It's okay," Matt answered. He wanted her to keep talking to him. "What's your name?" he asked, although he knew perfectly well what it was.

"Allie. Allison, really."

"Mine's Matt. Matt Tyson."

She stuck out her hand to shake. "Allison Behringer," she said fast, as if she wanted to get it over with.

"Like *Mr.* Behringer?" Matt asked.

"He's my father," Allie said.

"How come you're in your own father's class?"

"He wanted me to be. The school said it was all right as long as he didn't favor me. He goes the other way. I have to work harder. But I do like the way he teaches."

"Me, too." Matt nodded to emphasize his words.

"But a lot of the kids . . ."

"I know those kids," Matt said. "They always give teachers a hard time at first. They're okay, though, when they get to know you."

"The girls, too?" Allie asked. "We live way out in the boonies, so I only know the ones from the tiny little grade school I went to."

"I don't know about the girls," Matt said. He found himself being very honest with Allie, as though he could trust her not to tease. "I haven't known any of them really well since about second grade. Too much football, I guess." He smiled, then felt as though he looked stupid. But Allie smiled back, just naturally.

"You do play a lot, don't you?"

"I want to make the team. It's important."

"It must be," Allie said. "The boys talk about playing football, and the girls talk about the boys who play."

She made it sound sort of dumb. Matt didn't want her to think of him as just another jock, but he couldn't let her put him down.

"What's the matter with playing football? It's a great sport, and we do care about playing it well." His voice was angry.

It was Allie's turn to look embarrassed as the librarian shushed them.

"I know, I know," she whispered. "I never said there was anything the matter. I'd better do my math now."

Matt felt itchy and unsatisfied, but he, too, turned back to the math. He had finished all fifteen problems and begun on the grammar before study period was over. He walked slowly down the hall after Allie and watched her go up the stairs. He liked the way she moved, straight and strong. He caught up, taking the stairs two at a time. "See you in social studies tomorrow," he said.

"Right," Allie said. "So long."

Paul was waiting at the top of the stairs. "At least we have science together," he said, as they walked toward class. "You know that girl you were talking to just now? She's Behringer's kid."

"I know," Matt said. "She told me." There was something in his voice that made Paul look at him carefully.

"I just meant you should watch out what you say to her," Paul said hastily. "That's all."

Chapter Four

THE next day, Matt and Paul were early again, but the team list still wasn't up when they got there. Terry tried to look cool, but Matt got the impression that he might be getting a little nervous, too. Nobody said much as they stood around for a while, hoping Coach Wilson would post the list before class. They waited till the bell rang and they had to run for it. Matt slipped into his seat while Mr. Behringer was still writing on the board: Knights, Armor, Heraldry, Castles.

"Hi," Allie said, next to him. Matt grinned and said hi before Mr. Behringer began to talk. He found he couldn't listen very well. He wanted class to be over so he could go down and see if the list was posted. He tried to concentrate on what Mr. Behringer was saying about feudal obligations, the knight to protect vassals, the vassals to fight for the knight, but he drifted back into a daydream about catching a perfect pass from Paul. The scene was so vivid in his mind that Allie had to nudge him with her elbow twice before he realized that Mr. Behringer had called on him.

"Well, Matt, what do you choose? Are you still with us?" Mr. Behringer sounded calm, not sarcastic the way some teachers did when you were out of it. Matt blushed anyway.

"I'm sorry, I wasn't listening right then." He looked at the board to try to get an idea of what was going on. There were some new words now, and people's names written under some of them.

"All right, we'll come back to you," Mr. Behringer said, and called on Allie.

"The Children's Crusade," she said.

Mr. Behringer wrote Children's Crusade on the board, and her name under it.

"I want to work on Armor, too," Terry answered, when he was called on.

Mr. Behringer wrote his name on the board. There were two names under Armor now. So we're signing up to do reports, Matt thought. He remembered that Mr. Behringer had said they should think about what they'd like to work on, but he had read the social studies assignment on Friday, so he wouldn't have to do homework over the weekend. With the football tryout and thinking about the team, he'd completely forgotten about choosing a topic. Behringer was calling on the last two people, so he had to think fast.

"Want to do the Children's Crusade with me?" Allie asked softly. "People are supposed to pair up on these reports."

He looked at the board. Armor had two names under it. So did Weapons and Castles. He turned to Allie gratefully. "Sure," he said. "You want to?"

"Yes," she whispered, as Mr. Behringer called on Matt again.

"The Children's Crusade," Matt said firmly.

"Very good," Mr. Behringer said, smiling a little as he wrote Matt's name on the board under Allie's.

Matt realized that he didn't have any idea of what he'd gotten himself into. The Children's Crusade was just mentioned in one sentence in what they had read. He had been thinking about doing something about battle strategy and weapons. But he guessed it didn't really matter. And it might be fun to work with Allie. He hadn't done a project with a girl since second grade.

Mr. Behringer was talking again. "I want to give you the homework now because we're going to watch a movie for the rest of the period."

There was some clapping and cheers. Mr. Behringer ignored the noise and went on: "Read up to page fifty-six and answer the first three questions at the end of the chapter. In ink, please, and full sentences. And you'll need to start looking for books on your topics. You have to get information from two books besides the encyclopedia." Now there was a general groan from the students. Seventh grade was harder, no question.

"The movie we're going to see has nothing to do with the Middle Ages, but this was the only day I could get hold of it, and I thought you should see it. We'll spend our class time tomorrow discussing it. Some of it's pretty violent, I warn you."

"Oooo, I love violence," Terry teased, raising his arms like a vulture.

Mr. Behringer looked annoyed, but continued, "If any of you find you can't take it, you're free to leave. Just go quietly." He walked to the back of the room to operate the projector. "Turn off the lights, please, Tim," he said loudly, over the whispering and joking as the class tried to figure out what could be so violent.

Allie whispered to Matt, "It really is scary. I saw it last night at this meeting we went to." Matt started to ask her about it, but the movie began.

When he saw the huge mushroom cloud at the beginning, he understood. It was about Hiroshima in the days after the first atomic bomb, a movie made for a TV show that most of them hadn't seen. The worst part, Matt thought, was parents trying to find lost children, or children trying to find their parents. Some of them had been blinded by the flash of light as the bomb went off. All of them looked horribly burned. People and things closest to the center of the blast had just disappeared, without even leaving rubble or bones. In one place, you could see the outline of a person on a wall, like a photograph taken by the light of the explosion.

The movie lasted only twenty minutes, but in the middle, a few of the girls left. Mandy said loudly, "My dad says children shouldn't watch these things," but she stayed anyway. So did all of the boys. Even if they had wanted to leave, Matt thought, they had to prove they were tougher than the girls.

The bell rang while the movie was still going on, but everyone in the room stayed, silently, till it ended. There was a picture of pages being torn from a calendar, each page marked with a year up into the 1990s. The last picture was a cloud that started as a mushroom and changed into a question mark. Then it was over, and Mr. Behringer switched the lights on. Matt wanted a few seconds to recover before he had to talk to anyone. He had the same shivery feeling that seeing the missile had given him, only worse.

He looked at Allie. She was sitting there next to him, rubbing her eyes. He couldn't tell if she'd been crying. He wanted to tell her it had shocked him, too. "You okay?" he asked. "That was the saddest thing I ever saw."

"And scary, too," she said. They went out into the hall, still in a daze.

Paul ran up to them, waving his arms.

"Hurry up, Matt," he said. "Tom says the list's up. We've got to see it together!"

Matt tried to shake off the feeling of the movie and focus on Paul's words. Now Paul was yelling at Terry, too.

"Come on, we're going to be late, as it is," Paul urged. "What's with your class? You all look spacy."

"Tell you later," Matt said, suddenly back in the present. "Let's go." He and Paul and Terry ran to the stairs and jumped down most of them.

By the time they got to the bulletin board, there was already a small group of boys standing there, including Bobby Harneman, the eighth-grade quarterback, curious to see the new kids. "You made it, Terry," one of them yelled. Terry pushed through to see for himself, with Matt and Paul right behind him. The list was alphabetical, so Matt started from the bottom. Tyson was a name that was always nearly at the end. There it was! Tyson, Matthew. In clear, black, typed letters, so there could be no mistake.

Matt felt pure joy, better than any birthday or Christmas. He checked the list again and found Bondi, Paul. "We both made it," he yelled, turning to look at Paul, who was just standing there grinning.

Paul wrapped his arms around Matt's shoulders in a bear hug, and then they were both in the midst of the group, yelling and giving each other high fives. Matt pulled away and closed his eyes for a second. He just wanted to listen, and feel the amazing happiness inside himself.

"You okay?" Paul asked.

"Oh, sure," Matt said, smiling. "I can't believe it. I can't wait to tell my dad. I can't wait to play."

"Easy," Paul said. "We do have a little school to get through first. In fact, we better get back up to class. We're probably late enough to get detention, as it is."

"They wouldn't dare," Matt yelled, racing for the stairs. "We're the team."

In a way, he was right. At least for that morning, all the teachers gave them leeway to be late or noisy or distracted. They'd have to be normal again tomorrow, but today was special.

When Matt got to the lunch line in fifth period, Paul was still talking excitedly. "Hey, guys, you know that huge kid over there. . . ." He looked toward the very tall boy he'd pointed out to Matt at tryouts. "*He* didn't even make it."

"Tough," Terry said. "We're just too good."

Matt laughed. He couldn't imagine, right now, how it would feel if he hadn't made the team. It felt so good to be part of it, to be chosen, and twice as good to have Paul make it, too.

Sitting at "their" table, with the guys, it felt even better. He had been so worried, after Saturday, that he had tried not to let himself picture this scene. They were the top. They were the team! They were being loud and showing off, but if you were part of it, it didn't feel that way.

"Do you think Coach Wilson will let us choose what position we play?" Terry was asking.

"Don't be stupid," Paul said, with his mouth full of ham and cheese. "He puts you where he needs you." Paul was usually a neat eater, but he'd dropped the other half of his sandwich, and there was a smudge of mustard on his chin.

Terry went right on talking about how much better he could play at left tackle than at right, and Paul went right on answering with his mouth full. Matt watched and smiled, and even ate his crusts. The happiness was so deep, he felt as though he'd never be angry or disappointed again.

MATT got to the library for study hall before Allie did. He sat and watched her come in with two of the other seventh-grade girls. They were talking softly and seriously; he wished he could hear what they were saying. He wondered if they were talking about him. Then suddenly they all giggled. The other two sat down with Mandy, while Allie looked around for a seat and finally sat down next to him.

"What was so funny?" Matt asked, remembering to speak in the half whisper that the librarian seemed to allow.

"Oh, nothing," Allie said. But she smiled a little and then bit her lip, as though she were trying to keep from laughing out loud.

Matt liked the way she smiled. Her shiny dark hair fell like a curtain over the side of her face. He liked the way she brushed it back with her hand as she sat down.

He wanted to tell her about making the team, about how happy he felt, but he was afraid she'd think he was bragging. So he reached down to get the social studies book out of his knapsack.

"Are you sure we're going to be able to find out anything about this Children's Crusade?" he asked. "Our book only has about one sentence on it. And Behringer—I mean, your father—*Mr.* Behringer says we can't just use the encyclopedia." Matt thought for a second of how proud his father had been when he had bought an encyclopedia for him. "Now you can be smarter than I was," he'd said.

"Yeah, he's really down on them," Allie said. "He says we have to organize the information for ourselves."

"So we start with the card catalog," Matt said. At least he remembered library skills from last year. They went over to look it up together.

Allie began flipping through the C's. "There's children's practically everything, but not Children's Crusade." She turned back to the cards. There wasn't even a listing for Crusades.

"Let's try Middle Ages," Matt said.

There were two books and they found them on the shelf. But when they looked in each index, Children's Crusade was listed in only one of them. And when they got to the page, there was just one mention of it: "The Children's Crusade, a futile effort that resulted in the slaughter of many innocents, followed in 1212."

And that was all.

Matt was beginning to get annoyed. He hated trying to write reports when there was nothing to say. "Couldn't we write about something else?"

"Maybe we should try the town library first," Allie said. "My dad might drive us after school."

"I can't. I have to go to practice," Matt said. It felt so good to say it that he went on. "I made the football team, and first practice is this afternoon."

"I know," Allie said. "I mean, I know you made it. That's fantastic! Congratulations." She sounded as though she meant it.

"How did you know?" Matt asked.

"Oh, we have our ways," she said, teasing. "First of all, I could hardly miss it. . . . You guys have been three feet off the ground all day."

"But we've been waiting all this time to know. . . ." Matt began.

"I know," Allie said, more serious now. "I went down and looked at the list, too. I know it matters."

Matt looked at her to be sure she meant it, but she wasn't teasing anymore. He didn't know what had happened to make her understand how he felt, but she seemed to. He stood there, looking at her, until she said, "Well, what should we do?"

"What?" he asked. "Oh, yeah, about the report."

"Can you go to the library Saturday morning?" Allie asked.

"Make it afternoon," Matt said. "Saturday morning's still practice. That's when we usually have our games, but the first one's not for two weeks."

"There might be something in one of our books at home," Allie said. "I'll look."

Matt imagined her house all full of books, like a library. He wondered what it would be like to live with a teacher all the time. He didn't think he'd like it. Suddenly he was tired of the whole subject of the report. He wanted to get out of the library and out of school and back to football. He wanted, most of all, to tell his dad he'd made the team. He looked up to find Allie staring at *him* this time. He tried to remember what she'd just said. About books.

"Great, Allie. You look. And we'll do the library on Saturday afternoon." He turned and grabbed his books and was out the door, abruptly leaving Allie standing there for the second time that day.

WHEN football practice was over that afternoon, Matt and Paul rode home exhausted. Matt left his bike at the edge of the driveway and ran up the porch steps. "Mom," he yelled.

"Hi, Matt," she called. She came to meet him, smiling when she saw his happy, dirty face.

"I made it! We both did, Paul and me, I mean. It's so great. I couldn't believe it."

She hugged him. "That's wonderful. I know how much you wanted it. Come get some cookies and milk. You must be starving." As they walked toward the kitchen, he could smell oatmeal-chocolate-chip cookies, just baked. For as long as he could remember, she had baked them for special times, for celebration or for comfort. He bit into the first warm cookie, grateful that this time it was a celebration.

"Tell me how you found out. Was the list up when you all got there?"

He started to tell her about the list and Paul and Terry and practice, talking so fast and loud that he didn't hear his father come in.

"Hey, kid, you left your bike halfway in the driveway. I almost ran over it," he said.

Matt got up to put the bike away, but his father reached his hand out to stop him. "It's okay. I put it in the garage."

"Thanks. You mad?"

"Not really," he said. "I figured maybe you had a good reason for being in a hurry." He looked at Matt expectantly.

"I did. I made it, Dad, and . . ." His father had him in a bear hug before he could go on.

"Way to go, Matt. I knew you'd make it! Was practice this afternoon rough? I remember our coach nearly killed us that first day."

While Matt started to tell him, his mother handed him the plates and silverware to set the table, and they all sat down to dinner. Matt stopped talking and concentrated on eating. He was always starving after practice. His mom was talking about one of the kids at the nursery school where she taught. She had gone back to work when Matt was in fourth grade. His dad told about someone getting the address on an order mixed up, so that a little old lady on Elm

Street was astonished to find a truck in her driveway about to unload two tons of cement she'd never asked for. It all seemed absolutely ordinary, as though making the team had been a sure thing.

Matt felt so good, he didn't even mind when his father said that he had to go out to a meeting that night and couldn't stop to throw passes after dinner.

"That's okay, Dad. We'll have plenty of time now," he said, as coolly as he could.

"We sure will. It's going to be some fun watching those games!"

Matt didn't think much about the meeting his father was going to. There were always lots of meetings early in the fall, when everyone was getting back into regular activities after the summer. In fact, his mom had gone to a meeting the night before at her friend Jan's house. She hadn't said anything about it at breakfast that morning, so Matt guessed it hadn't been anything he'd be interested in.

His dad was going off to his veterans' club meeting. It was just an informal club. A group of the men he'd grown up with and later gone to war with belonged to it. Matt knew some of them from Little League football, where they coached different teams. The club always had a picnic and fireworks on the Fourth of July. Matt didn't know what they did the rest of the time, but he knew his father enjoyed being part of it.

Matt sat down to finish his homework after dinner, but he felt too restless to study. He decided to call Paul.

"You still feeling great?" he asked.

"Yeah, except I can't get the last three math problems," Paul said.

Matt talked Paul through them, then asked impulsively, "Hey, did you ever work on a report with a girl?"

"I don't think so," Paul said. "I don't remember for sure. How come?"

Matt explained how he'd forgotten to choose a topic, and how Allie had sort of rescued him.

"I don't think you can get out of it now," Paul said.

"I know. I mean, I don't really *want* to get out of it. Allie's smart . . ."

"Yeah, and her father's the teacher, too."

"What's that supposed to mean?"

"C'mon, Matt, don't be dense. It means a good mark, that's what."

"I don't know. Maybe teachers have to be specially tough on their own kids, like Allie says. Anyway, that's not the thing. I don't exactly know how to act."

Paul thought for a second. "Act natural, I guess. I mean, you can't pretend she's a guy, but just get the work done."

Matt paused for a minute and then took a chance. "The trouble is, when I look at her, I get distracted."

Paul started humming "Love's Got Me Going," the song that was on the radio that summer every time they turned it on.

Matt was sorry he'd said anything. Quickly, he asked Paul if he'd found out whether he could go with them on the camping trip.

"Oh, sure. I just forgot to tell you. My mom wants to know how cold it's going to get, and how are we going to stay dry if it rains, and . . ."

Matt started to laugh. Paul's mother was famous for worrying about every tiny detail. "I guess my dad'll figure it out, as usual. It's good you can come, though. See you tomorrow."

When his father came home at about ten-thirty, Matt was in bed and half-asleep. He heard him talking very loudly in the kitchen, and his mother answering calmly. Then he heard her say, "Can't it wait till morning?" as his father thumped down the hall toward Matt's room. Matt sat up in bed as the door opened.

"Oh, good, you're awake," Mr. Tyson said. He switched on the light next to Matt's bed. "Did you see a movie in school today?" he asked.

Matt had to go back over the day for a minute to remember, and then he nodded. It was strange to think that he'd almost forgotten about the movie, when it had been so horrifying at the time. Football had wiped it out, he thought a little guiltily.

"About Hiroshima?" his father was asking.

"Yes," Matt said. "About the first atomic bomb and what happened to people afterward." He shook his head. "It was pretty awful."

"Right," his father said. "And I heard some of the girls were crying, and one actually felt so sick the school nurse sent her home."

"I didn't know about that," Matt said.

"And it was part of class? You had to watch it?"

"Yes," Matt said. "I mean no. Wait. Behringer said we could leave if we wanted to."

"Behringer. He's the one," his father said. "What right does he have to show you kids a movie like that? Without even letting parents know?"

The anger in his father's voice was reflected in his flushed face. Even though Matt knew his father wasn't angry at him, he felt defensive.

"Hey, Dad, it was just a movie, and they said it was on TV before. How come you're so mad?"

"Sure, just a movie. But this was in school. And now there's going to be *just* another protest. A sit-in. Women and children lying down in the road to keep more missiles from getting to the army base! And that Behringer is trying to brainwash you kids."

Mrs. Tyson, who had been standing at the door, interrupted her husband. "Wait a minute, that's not fair, and it's not like you. You just got carried away by the guys at your meeting."

Matt's father turned to look at her. "How do you know?" he asked. "You weren't there."

"No, but I did see the movie. They showed it at the meeting I went to *last* night." Matt did a double take. That was what Allie had said. So it must have been the same meeting, he thought.

His father still sounded angry. "Oh. How come you didn't tell me about it?"

"Remember, it was kind of late when I got back? I said I'd tell you all about the meeting in the morning. Then I was so busy I guess I forgot."

"Or maybe you knew I'd be mad."

"Maybe that, too," Mrs. Tyson said.

Matt listened tensely to his parents not quite fighting, but on the edge of it. It made him nervous.

"So that was the meeting to plan the protest?" his father went on. "And that guy Behringer was there, too, right?"

"Look," she said, calmly. "Jan wanted me to come, at least to see that movie. And I'm glad I did. Everybody should see it."

"Oh? And I suppose now you're going to go sit

down in the road, too, and keep the missile trucks from going through? Isn't that why they showed the movie?"

Matt's mother shook her head and tried to explain, but her husband interrupted her.

"You know, a couple of the guys at the club were so mad they wanted to take guns to scare people away from the protest."

"Oh, no. They wouldn't."

"No, they wouldn't. C'mon, they're sane, and most of the guys listened when I said guns would likely cause trouble. But they were mad." He shook his head. "What we decided is we're going to go watch to make sure nothing bad *does* happen, to try to keep things peaceful."

"All right, but no guns," Mrs. Tyson said.

"No. But I'll tell you there's some bad feeling here. They say outsiders are running the protest and causing all this trouble for us. Anyway, you're an adult, you can make up your own mind. But I wish Matt weren't in Behringer's class."

"But, Dad, he's a great teacher. Even the Middle Ages isn't boring. You want me to be bored to death like Paul in Mrs. Garth's class? And besides, we've already signed up to do reports and I'm working with—" He stopped just in time, but his dad wasn't really listening anyway.

"See?" Mr. Tyson looked at his wife. "The kid's brainwashed already. I want him out of that class."

Matt was stunned. Could his father really mean it? he wondered.

Then his mother was speaking, very calmly and quietly. "Johnny, I know you want to do what's best. You said you argued against the guys who wanted to take guns to scare the protesters. Now you're sounding like them. Behringer's got a right to teach. Matt's old enough to learn to think for himself. And seeing a movie about what really happened when the bomb went off won't brainwash him. Let's cool off and talk about this in the morning."

Matt watched his father listen, take a deep breath, and suddenly grin at his wife. "All right," he said. "Maybe I got a little brainwashed myself." He looked over at Matt. "Sorry I got you up, kid. We'll talk in the morning. Sleep well."

Matt listened to them going down the hall to their room to see whether they started arguing again. No. They could stop, just like that, as if they hadn't really been angry.

Still, he was glad he hadn't said he was doing his report with Allie. He wondered how angry his dad would be if he knew. It would be weird to make trouble over something that happened just by accident because he hadn't remembered to choose a report topic in time.

He didn't feel at all sleepy, but he lay down again and tried to think about something else. Football was usually safe, running plays in his head. And this time there was no worry. He had made the team. He smiled and pictured himself running hard, turning just in time to catch Paul's bullet pass.

Chapter Five

EVERYTHING *did* seem normal again in the morning. His dad didn't even mention the movie or the protest when Matt went off to school.

In social studies they discussed Hiroshima, so everyone got a chance to say how awful nuclear war would be, but seeing the movie didn't seem to have changed anyone's ideas about missiles one way or the other. Mr. Behringer made sure they listened to each other. Then it was back to the Middle Ages.

Football practice seemed to get tougher each afternoon. On Thursday, even Chris Clum, the eighth-grader they called Truck, had to walk his bike uphill on the way home. Paul, Matt, and Chris sprawled on his front lawn with cold sodas and popcorn for a few minutes before Matt and Paul rode the extra mile home.

When Matt got up for more popcorn, Paul tripped him and Matt stuffed a handful in Paul's mouth. Suddenly Bobby Harneman was there, too. "All right, team!" he said as he came up to take the soda Chris offered.

"We better get home," Matt said, not wanting to look too silly in front of the eighth-grade quarterback.

On Friday, when Mr. Behringer reminded the class about turning in a list of books for their reports, Allie asked Matt if he remembered about going to the town library after Saturday-morning practice.

"Let's meet at twelve-thirty," he said. "No problem."

Saturday's practice ended by noon, and Matt got to the library before Allie did. He stood inside the entry looking at the bulletin board while he waited.

There was all the usual stuff about Books Needed for the Veterans' Hospital, Fire Department Rescue Show and Pot Luck Supper, Exercise Classes for Toddlers and Moms. Then the word *missiles* caught his eye. Protest Against Missiles, the notice began, and he stopped to read it carefully.

"Missiles spell D–A–N–G–E–R, not S–T–R–E–N–G–T–H," it said, in big green letters.

"Join us Saturday, October 19, to protest nuclear missile storage here in Hancock. *Don't let our town be a target*. Keep Hancock safe for children and other living things." At the bottom it said, "Planning Meeting: Monday, September 12, 8 P.M., 22 Hickory Street. Women's Campaign for a Nuclear-free Environment."

It didn't sound as though they were inviting kids, but they would certainly know a lot about the missiles at the army base. He looked at the date again and realized, annoyed, that it had been *last* Monday. It was the meeting where his mother and Allie had seen the movie about the bomb.

At that moment, Allie ran up the steps. "Sorry I'm late," she began. "You know we live too far outside town to bike, so I had to wait for my mom, and she took years getting ready."

"That's okay," Matt said, hardly listening to her apology. "It doesn't matter. Read this." He pointed to the poster and she read it quickly.

"Yeah, there's going to be a protest. They want as many people as they can possibly get," she said. "That's what they told us at that meeting."

"Did they talk about the missiles at the base?"

"Sure," Allie said. "They said the army wants to store them here because this is a good place to launch them over the north pole, if we ever get attacked."

Matt nodded. "What else?"

"Mostly they talked about how nuclear missiles could destroy the earth forever, and how much we don't want them here 'cause they make this town a target."

"I wish I'd been there," Matt said. She sounds so sure of herself, he thought, and turned toward the inside of the library. "We better get going on the report."

"Yeah, my mom said she'd be back for me in an hour."

It didn't take that long. There was nothing on the Children's Crusade, even though Allie was terrific at thinking of other things to look under. Matt got pretty good at it himself. But even going through Medieval, Jerusalem, and Holy War, they found only three books that had any decent Crusade information, and still hardly a word about the Children's Crusade. It was better than what was available at school, but not enough to write more than a page.

"Let's try the encyclopedia now," Matt said impatiently. They got a few more bits of information.

But Allie looked determined. "Let's ask the librarian while we're waiting."

"She'll just tell us to look in the card catalog again. It's a dumb topic anyway," he muttered.

But he followed Allie as she went over to ask. The librarian looked at the books they'd found. "You've done pretty well," she said. "It *is* a hard thing to find out about. Did you check the bibliographies?"

Allie blushed and shook her head.

The librarian looked in the back of each of the books. She went so fast they could hardly follow. Finally she stopped and pointed: "Gray, George Z., *The Children's Crusade.*"

"Great," Matt said, "but it isn't here."

"I may be able to get it for you," she said. "How much time do you have?" Matt looked at Allie.

"I guess we could wait a few days," she said.

"I'll try to get it through the interlibrary loan service. The state university's included, so they probably have it somewhere. Let me check." She dialed a three-digit number and talked briefly to the person who answered. "They do have it," she said. "We're awfully lucky to get it on the first try." Matt thought she sounded as though she'd just caught a big fish. "Come back next Wednesday or call me here. I'll ask them to rush."

"Thanks," Allie said. "Thanks a lot."

As they left her desk, Matt asked, "What if she can't get that book and we have to choose something else? Will your dad mark us late?"

"No special favors," Allie said. "But he'll be psyched about the interlibrary thing. And she said she'd get it by Wednesday. We could pick it up on Saturday."

They walked to the steps to wait for Allie's mother.

"Is your mom always late?" Matt asked.

"Not *really* late," Allie said. "It's like she gets interested in what she's doing and forgets what time it is."

"Does she have a job?"

"Sort of. She's an artist," Allie said.

"Like paintings in a museum?"

"Not quite," Allie said, smiling. "She does illustrations for children's books."

"That's neat."

"How about *your* mom?" Allie asked.

"She teaches nursery school in the mornings. Maybe she reads the kids books with your mom's illustrations." He leaned back against the library steps. The sun was warm now, and he felt good talking to Allie. He found out that she was an only child, too, and that her family had lived in Boston for a while, and then New York, before her parents decided they wanted a different kind of life.

"Don't you miss New York?" Matt asked.

"In a way," Allie answered. "I still miss my

friends. And I miss being able to go visit just by walking a couple of blocks or getting on a crosstown bus."

"You were allowed to go on a bus by yourself?" Matt asked. "Weren't you afraid of getting mugged?"

Allie laughed. "Well, once some kids did steal my bus pass. But that was the only bad thing that happened. My parents didn't let me go alone till I was nine, so I only had a bit of it before we came here."

Matt looked at Allie hard. She had seemed so shy at first, not quite knowing how to manage in middle school. And yet she knew how to get around by herself in New York City. That made *him* feel shy. He wanted her to keep on talking, but they sat there quietly for a few minutes.

"Are you going to be quarterback on the football team?" Allie asked at last.

"Not quarterback," Matt answered. "I'm a receiver. I like to catch the ball. Paul's going to be quarterback."

"You've got it all planned."

Matt shrugged. "Not exactly planned. Hoped for is more like it."

"From the time you were a little kid, I bet. Did your dad teach you?"

Matt started to tell her about his father, about how he'd led the Wayne County team when he was in school, and how that made football something important between them. She listened intently, watching his face as he talked. He felt as though she really cared. He was going to tell her about Vietnam, too, and his dad's leg, but he thought maybe it would make her pity his father—and he didn't want that. Maybe when he knew her better, he thought.

"I'd like to see you play," Allie said.

"Come to the game next Saturday. I don't know if Coach Wilson will let any seventh-graders play yet, but he might."

"I'll try," Allie said. "We could go get the book after the game, too."

As she said it, her mother came up the library steps. She was wearing blue jeans and running shoes, and her hair, long and straight like Allie's, was in a thick braid down her back. She looked very young.

"Hey, you two. Didn't you hear me beeping?"

"Sorry, Mom," Allie said. Matt stood up. "Mom, this is Matt Tyson. Who I'm doing the report with."

Mrs. Behringer smiled. "Hi, Matt. You guys seem to have chosen a tough subject. Good luck." She turned to Allie. "C'mon, honey. I've got to get back."

Matt stood on the library steps and watched them drive away. Then he got his bike and rode home as

67

fast as he could. He remembered that Paul was coming over, so they could go to the senior high school game that afternoon, the way they had done all last year. Matt wondered what he would do next week if Allie came to their game. How was he going to make it to the library after the game and still meet Paul? He decided not to worry about that till it happened. Like his mom said, sometimes the thing you worried about never did happen.

Chapter Six

THE day of the first game, Matt and Paul sat next to each other on the bench, watching intently as the team lined up after the kickoff. All of the boys on the field were eighth-graders.

"Do you think we'll ever get a chance to play?" Paul asked. "Those guys look even better than they did in practice."

"We will, sometime," Matt said, still watching the field. "But Coach Wilson isn't going to fool around in the first game. Not against Washington Township. They're too good. You heard him this morning."

It had been a real pep talk, like the ones in the movies. "Winning once is more than half of winning

69

twice," the coach had said. "It's intimidation. It knocks out the confidence of the next team we play."

Matt and Paul had listened, silent, fists clenched, half-scared, half-excited. At the end of the speech, the whole team yelled and gave each other high fives before running out on the field. Matt would have liked to duck into the bathroom one last time, but he didn't dare. Besides, he'd already peed three times since breakfast, so he knew he didn't really have to.

It was nervousness, that was all. Just sitting on the bench didn't help. He still felt tense and wished he could get up and run around to get rid of the feeling. He started to stand up and then thought that he didn't want the coach to notice him that way. And he didn't want to be teased about being nervous.

He watched Bobby Harneman throw a twenty-yard pass to Ken Akers for a first down. He tried to judge honestly whether he could have caught it. He thought he could. Bobby wasn't as strong as Matt's father, of course. But he was dead accurate. The ball seemed to slide right into Ken's hands. Matt wished he'd get a chance to play.

Paul was nudging him. "Do you still feel nervous?" he asked.

"Not so much," Matt said.

"Me neither," Paul said. "I want a chance to throw like that. I think I could."

Matt nodded, looking at the field again. The team

was on the seventeen-yard line, and Bobby had handed off the ball to Chris Clum. Matt remembered that Chris had been teased and called Clum-sy when he'd played in Little League. Nobody called him that anymore. Chris ran around two tackles, out into the open, and over the line for a touchdown. Matt stood up and cheered with the rest of the team.

He looked around behind him where the cheer-leaders were doing cartwheels on the running track in front of the stands. Everybody on their side of the field was up and yelling. Matt spotted his father and mother right at the fifty-yard line, but he couldn't see Allie. He wondered if she had come.

And then he saw her, at the near end of the stands, way up in back, standing up like everyone else, but not yelling. She seemed to be with one other girl, a little taller than she was, whom Matt didn't recognize. He turned to Paul. "Who's that girl with Allie?"

Paul turned to look. "Where?" he asked. "I don't even see Allie."

"Up at the top of the stands," Matt said. Then, looking again, he realized that it must be Allie's mother. He couldn't imagine that she was interested in a middle school football game. She and Allie were talking and looking down at the team. Then suddenly Allie pointed at him and waved. Matt waved back and then, feeling a little silly, turned back to Paul and the game.

71

Still, it made him feel good to think that she had been looking for him. Now he wanted to play more than ever. He wanted her to see how good he could be. He wanted her to see what it meant.

The team kicked off and she sat down. Not for long, though. Ken Akers intercepted the Washington team's pass and ran back for another touchdown. Matt cheered for Ken and for the team. He turned to look at Paul. "Maybe now," Matt said. "It's a pretty good lead."

The more they were ahead, the more chance there was that Coach Wilson might let some of the seventh-graders play. But it didn't happen until they were twenty-six to six in the fourth quarter.

There was a time out, and Coach Wilson looked down the bench to where the seventh-graders were sitting. "Okay, Terry, you give Clum a rest. Matt, go in for Ken Akers."

Matt stood up and pulled on his helmet. He started onto the field fast, wanting the coach to see how ready he was. He turned back for just a second to look at Paul, still sitting on the bench with his face set in a half squint, half smile. For a moment Matt felt bad that Paul wasn't beside him, running onto the field. But the team was getting into a huddle, and Bobby Harneman was announcing the play that Coach wanted next.

"I'm going back to pass, to Jim or to Matt, whichever of you gets free. It'll probably be Matt, 'cause he's new, and Washington'll be guarding Jim hard."

Matt listened carefully as Bobby went over the counts for the play. Bobby slapped him on the shoulder as they left the huddle.

Matt didn't have time to be nervous. He had to concentrate to hear Bobby's signals, and then, as he ran through the opening he saw between two defenders, he felt as though he were running in a cloud. He didn't hear anything except the counting in his mind. He was in the clear, and he turned to see the ball coming at him, just as though his dad had thrown it. Bobby was so accurate he only had to move sideways a foot, and the ball was in his hands, tight against his chest.

Then he was running again, chased by a Washington linebacker and their safety, who'd suddenly seen where the ball was going. He got another ten yards before the safety brought him down, hard. But he held the ball, feeling it safe against his body. As the safety gave him a hand to get up, he thought he could hear his father saying, "Only the ball, always the ball," right inside his head. And he'd done it. He'd caught the ball and held it, in a real game. He heard cheering, but he felt so good already that it hardly mattered.

As he ran back to the huddle, he turned for just a second to look for Allie. She was at the top of the stands, waving and yelling. Coach Wilson left Matt in for the next two plays, and he concentrated hard on his job of blocking the opposing cornerback. He knew he wouldn't get anything so wonderful to do again, but he wanted to do the regular things just right. And he did. He couldn't believe his luck. As he came out of the game, his face was red from running. He could feel it get still redder when Coach slapped him on the shoulder and said, "Nice run, Tyson, way to go."

Matt walked back down the bench to sit next to Paul. Paul looked at him, still half-smiling. "You really looked good," he said.

"Thanks." Matt would have liked to show Paul how much he wanted him to get his chance, but Paul was already looking back at the game. I'll say something later, Matt thought. Maybe he'll still get a chance.

Paul did, the next time they got the ball. They were ahead thirty-two to six. The coach called to Paul, "Okay, Bondi, you go in for Harneman."

Paul jumped up, fastening the strap on his helmet as he ran over to Coach Wilson to get the plays. He hurried onto the field and into the huddle. The first play was a run for a first down. Then it was a pass play.

Paul faded back, set, and looked downfield. Matt felt like yelling "Hurry up, throw it," as he watched Paul hesitate, and saw the opposing tackle coming up on his blind side. It was too late. Paul was sacked. He got up slowly, but at least he still had the ball. He called the signals to try again. This time he threw faster, but the pass was incomplete.

As the team went back into the huddle again, Matt wished he were there. He knew Paul must be feeling horrible, and he thought he could calm him down, make him do his best. But there was no way. Paul bobbled the snap from the center and barely held onto the ball, taking a loss on the play. The final play had to be a punt, giving up the ball to the other team.

Paul came off the field, head down, not speaking.

Matt put his arm over Paul's shoulder, and they sat that way until the final whistle two minutes later. Mandy and the other cheerleaders were on the field, doing a last fancy cheer, pom-poms and all. Matt's father and mother were there next to him, hugging and congratulating him.

"Way to go, kid," his father said.

"My two football heroes," his mother added, putting her arms around both of them.

Matt felt a little embarrassed. He was ready to go back to the locker room with the other guys and hear what Coach Wilson had to say about the game.

I'll think of a way to make Paul feel better, he thought. And then we'll go to the high school game together, the way we always do.

He had forgotten all about Allie—but suddenly, there she was.

"You were fantastic," she said, sounding a little shy. Her mother was there, too.

"Thanks. Thanks for coming." Matt didn't know what else to say. "I've got to change now. I'll see you," he said.

"Do you want me to pick up the book at the library?" Allie asked. "Mom said she'd drive back to town." Matt felt guilty and a little irresponsible, but all he wanted to do now was to be with the team, and especially with Paul.

"Listen," he said, trying to think. "Coach Wilson says we have a meeting when we're all changed." It was a lie, but it seemed to sound true enough. "I didn't know about it until today." He thought he'd better stop before it sounded too much like an alibi. "I don't know how long it'll take and then I promised to go up to the high school game with Paul. . . ."

Allie blushed and nodded.

"I'm sorry," Matt said.

"Oh, that's okay," Allie said. "I can get the book myself. But do you want to work on the report tomorrow?"

"Definitely," Matt said, glad of the chance to redeem himself a little. "What if I get Mom to drive me out to your place? What time?"

"Twelve?"

"Fine," Matt said. "I'll see you then. Crow Hill Road, right?"

"Right," Allie said. "See you."

As she turned away, she took her mother's hand, looking very young. Matt watched, sorry to have made her feel bad. He'd try to make up for it tomorrow. Then he turned and ran toward the locker room.

Chapter Seven

THE sun was at the center of a blazing blue fall sky when Matt and his mother drove to the top of Crow Hill Road. There was only one house visible, set back just a little from the road, looking south down the valley.

"What an incredible view," Mrs. Tyson said. "I can see why they'd want to live out here."

Matt was already halfway out of the car, checking the name on the mailbox just to make sure. BEHRINGER was so beautifully painted, white on very dark blue, it looked as if it had been done by a machine. Then Matt remembered that Allie's mother was an artist. He heard his mother saying something.

"What?"

"I said, Call me when you're ready to be picked up. We'll be home all afternoon."

He went back to shut the door on his side of the car. "Thanks, Mom."

As he turned toward the house, Allie was on the porch, waving. He had been afraid she might be mad about the day before, but she was smiling. He walked up the short path, looking around at the weathered barn off to the right, beyond the driveway.

"Hi, Allie," he said. "Hey, do you have animals in that barn?"

"Two goats. C'mon, I'll show you."

The goats were outside, in a pen in back of the barn. They were grayish brown with little beards and soft brown eyes.

"Can I pet them?" Matt asked. "Do they bite or anything?"

"They just sort of nibble with their lips, but they don't bite," Allie said, opening the gate of the pen.

Matt liked the feel of their rough fur and the way they butted him softly, wanting attention.

"They like to have their heads scratched." She showed him.

Matt tried it. "I thought they were supposed to smell, or something."

"Not if you take care of them right," Allie said. "I go to 4-H Club meetings once a month to find out stuff like that."

"Is it hard?" He suddenly imagined himself with two goats in the backyard at home. Maybe they would eat the grass and he wouldn't have to mow the lawn.

"Milking them is hard at first, and trimming their hooves. Dad helps with that."

"You milk them yourself?" Matt asked.

"Mom does it in the morning, and I do it in the afternoon. You can try it later, if you want."

Matt nodded, impressed.

"We should start on the report, I guess," Allie said. "Are you hungry? Mom made sandwiches for us."

Matt nodded again and followed her out of the pen and back to the house. As Allie opened the door, he felt as if he'd walked into a rainbow. There wasn't much furniture—one squashy-looking couch and two chairs in the living room, a round table and four chairs in the huge kitchen-dining room. But there were paintings hanging on the walls wherever there was space. In one sunny window there were shelves holding glasses and bottles in deep reds and blues and greens. The light coming through them made what looked like another painting on the floor. Everywhere he looked there were books, shelves and shelves of them, just as he had imagined.

Allie's father was sitting on the couch, reading

the Sunday paper, just the way his father did. It was weird seeing his teacher at home.

"Hi, Matt," he said. "Allie says you were terrific in the game yesterday."

"I was lucky, I guess," Matt said awkwardly. "It was fun."

"I'll bet," Mr. Behringer said, smiling and going back to the paper. "I was never any good at that."

Allie and Matt got the sandwiches and took them out to the sunny front porch. Matt was grateful not to have to try to talk to Mr. Behringer anymore.

"Can I see the book?" Matt said.

Allie handed it to him. "The librarian said we were lucky. This is some kind of classic or something."

"Did you read it already?"

"Just to the end of the introduction," Allie said.

"Let me read that, so I know what you know. Then we can read the rest together."

Matt quickly read the introduction, which said that the Children's Crusade was barely mentioned even in medieval records, and that historians had generally ignored it.

"That's certainly true," Matt commented aloud. "Look at the trouble we had trying to find out about it." He took a bite of his sandwich.

"What?" Allie asked, and read over his shoulder. "But it goes on to say that what happened was really sort of extraordinary. Anyway, read fast. I'll get the cookies. You want milk or juice?"

"Milk." He didn't even look up from the book. He had nearly finished the introduction by the time she came back. When he shut the book, she handed him his milk and watched him take a sip.

"Oooh, weird," he said. "Goat's milk?" It tasted like the goats smelled—a little sharp—and not as sweet as cow's milk.

She grinned. "It's okay. I'll get you some regular milk. My dad doesn't like goat either."

"Are you drinking it?"

"Yeah," Allie said, "but I'm used to it."

"If you can, I can," he said. He turned back to the book, feeling he ought to start doing his share. "Let's go through what we know now, so we can see what we have to find out, okay? We're in the summer of 1212, right?"

"Right."

"They've tried four Crusades and they haven't worked and tons of people have been killed. Right?"

"Right," Allie said again, getting into the rhythm of it.

"Pope Innocent III is trying to persuade everyone that this is the last chance to save the Holy Land from the infidels." He turned to her. "What exactly is an infidel?"

"My dad made me look it up. The dictionary says it's someone who doesn't believe in a particular religion, especially Christianity. Here they mean the Moslems—you know, the Arabs who lived all around Jerusalem and thought the Christians were devils."

"So they were fighting about religion?" Matt asked.

"I guess so. About religious places anyway. The Christians wanted Jerusalem because that's where Christ died, and the Moslems wanted it because of something about Mohammed."

"So they were really fighting for a place, after all."

"Kind of," she agreed.

They stretched out on their stomachs, side by side on the warm boards of the porch, the book in front of them. Matt liked lying beside Allie in the sun, but they were careful not to bump into each other. He had been finished with the first page for a few seconds when Allie said, "Ready?"

"Ready," he answered.

"You're a fast reader," Allie said.

"You, too. But I guess I expected that."

They read on for half an hour. They had already found that most of the children never got back home, that they starved or were sold into slavery. Matt still didn't understand what made them go. Then they read about Stephen, a twelve-year-old French shepherd boy who believed that the man who persuaded him to lead a Crusade was really Jesus Christ. They learned that children all over France believed Stephen enough to follow him. The author wrote that many of the children just wanted to get away from their hard lives at home.

"How did they think they were going to fight grown-up men?" Matt asked.

"Wait," Allie said, reading on. "They weren't going to fight. They thought they could convert the Moslems to being Christian."

"Fat chance," Matt said. "It's pretty hard to make people change what they believe in."

They read on for a few minutes. "Never mind what they were going to do when they got there," Allie said. "They thought the Mediterranean Sea was going to split apart so they could walk across to Jerusalem!"

"It must have been strange to believe so much," Matt said thoughtfully.

"I know," Allie agreed. "But they didn't really have anything else. I mean, they didn't go to school, most of them. Practically nobody could read. How could they know anything?"

"Still, it's weird." He got up to stretch for a minute, looking out over the valley. Allie sat up and went on reading to herself. Matt looked down at her. Then, reluctantly, feeling as though he had to keep doing his share, he sat down again.

"Listen," she said. "Here's another neat thing. They sang all the time they were walking. People would hear them coming before they could see them."

"Like that first protest march. My dad and I were throwing passes when we heard it. Were you in it, Allie?" he asked.

"Mmm, but I didn't really know why then."

He stood up again. "We've got enough stuff here to write five reports," he said. "I was afraid we were going to have to bull the whole thing."

Allie got up and sat on the porch step. "Want to stop for a while? I'll show you our hill where the view of the mountains is really good."

"Sure," Matt said. "We've done enough for now." He followed her down the steps and around the back of the house. A kind of wagon track led up the side of the steep slope. They moved fast, not exactly competing, but neither wanting to go slower than the other. They were a little out of breath when they got to the top.

"Look," Allie said. "My father says you can see into Vermont down that way. And up into Canada in the other direction."

Matt nodded and followed where her finger pointed. There were mountains, all right, miles of them, turning blue and misty in the distance.

"That way," she said, turning him around a little and pointing.

"And that way?" Matt asked, pointing straight up into the sky. When Allie lifted her head to look, he tickled her under the chin with a piece of straw he'd picked up.

"Hey, no fair," Allie said, brushing away the straw and half-tackling him. He shook her off lightly, trying to keep from touching too hard, and they both tumbled gently to the ground.

"Did you ever try this?" she asked quickly. She began to roll down the hill, her arms folded to protect her face from the rough grass. She stopped for a moment to see whether he was following her.

Matt rolled down to where she was. "Sure, we used to have picnics on the other side of the lake. I would roll all the way down and jump in the water."

"Sounds neat. Sometimes I wish I'd grown up here, too." She was quiet for a minute. "I still feel a little bit different, like a city girl."

"How?"

"Somehow up here people seem quieter, not so bigmouthed and teasy as in New York. I really had to watch myself at first. Now I feel right when I just act natural."

When Allie talked about herself like that, he felt close enough to ask the question that had been bothering him since the day before. "Allie, are you mad about yesterday?"

"I was embarrassed, with my mother there and all. I mean, I sort of dragged her to the game, and then . . ." She sounded annoyed.

"I'm sorry."

"I know. You *had* to be with the team."

"'Specially Paul," he said, "till he stopped feeling so bad. We've been practicing together for a long time, and he didn't really get a chance to look good, and I . . ." He stopped, not wanting to brag.

"I know," she repeated, smiling. "It feels good to get it right. Like the goats—when Nellie-goat won the ribbon for best-groomed, I was so proud. Not for the prize, but for learning how to do it."

"Like that," he agreed. "Hey, you said you'd show me how to milk that prize goat."

"It's a tiny bit early, but I guess we could." She got up and started to walk toward the barn. He stood slowly, looking out over the valley. The distant lines of the mountains under the blue sky were beautiful in a way he wanted to remember. He had felt sorry for Allie, living so far outside town. It had seemed lonely. Now he understood why her family would want to be there. He turned and followed her to the barn.

Her father was inside, moving blocks of hay into the feeding rack at the edge of the goats' pen.

"Want some help?" Matt asked.

"Thanks. I'm about done," Mr. Behringer said. "Let Allie show you how to milk them."

Allie had nudged one of the goats over to the milking stand. She got the goat's front feet up on a block.

"Why do you do that?" Matt asked.

"They kick. This way she can't knock over the pail with her hind legs." She sat down on a little stool and began to milk. A steady stream of milk rattled into the pail.

"Can I try?"

"Sure. Sit down." She got up and stood behind him.

He tried to copy what Allie had done, but only a few drops of milk came out. "Show me again," he said.

Allie reached over and showed him how to press with each finger in succession. "It only looks like I'm pulling. Try it again."

He did and got a few drops more, but there still wasn't even a trickle. "C'mon, you stubborn goat," he muttered. Allie giggled. Matt didn't mind that so much, but he didn't want to look dumb in front of Mr. Behringer, who had come over to watch. The goat stamped one of her back feet, as if she were impatient. Allie sat down to finish.

"It's okay, Matt," Mr. Behringer said, shaking his head and smiling. "I still can't do it as well as Allie and her mother can, and I've been trying since we moved here. We thought Allie might be lonely, so we got the goats right away." He picked up the pail of milk to carry it to the house, as Allie led the goat back inside the pen. "How're you coming on the report?" he asked. "It looks like you've got hold of the right book."

"It *is* good," Matt said. "I was afraid we weren't going to find anything."

"Mmm, and you don't seem to like not knowing."

Matt looked at him inquiringly.

"I mean, about goats or Crusades or missiles or anything." He sounded as though he approved.

That was good, at least. Matt still wondered whether he'd looked like a teacher's pet, when he had gone to see Mr. Behringer in the classroom, right at the beginning of school, and if he did now, working with Allie. He hoped not.

She trotted up beside him. "We should go back and do the outline, I guess."

It had gotten a little cooler as the sun started to set, and she and Matt sat at the table inside, taking turns reading and making notes. They decided they'd each write half the sections and put the report together the next weekend.

"On *Sunday*, of course," Allie said.

Matt looked at his watch. "I guess I'd better call my mom to come and get me."

She showed him where the telephone was. As he hung up, Allie asked, "Is your game at home or away this week?"

"Away. It usually alternates. Want to come? They have a bus from school."

"Maybe I will. There's only one time I really can't. But that's not till October."

"What's happening then?"

"The protest. On the nineteenth. Remember the poster? We're going to sit down on the road in front of the army base, so they can't bring the rest of the missiles in."

"They're really going to let kids do that, too?"

"Sure, we're people."

Matt realized that he hadn't been thinking about the missiles much since he'd made the football team. "I guess if I hate them so much I should go protest, too," he said, thinking aloud.

"You can't," Allie said. "Remember? It's on a Saturday morning. You'll be playing."

Of course he would. There was no way Coach

Wilson was going to excuse him for one game. He had made it clear: Anyone who didn't show up for a game had better have a swear-on-the-Bible excuse or forget football for that year.

"I wish I could," he said. "But there's no way I can skip one Saturday morning and stay on the team." He didn't like the way he sounded, like when a grown-up said, "I wish I could let you do that," when you knew they really didn't.

"Hey, Matt, it's okay," Allie reassured him.

He felt almost put down, like a little kid who'd spilled a glass of milk. But he couldn't stop. "And my dad would never understand my giving up a chance to play. Especially for a protest."

"The protest doesn't seem too popular around here anyway," Allie said sharply. "Someone sent an anonymous letter to my dad telling him he'd better get out."

"You're kidding!"

"I'll show you. He took it to the police, but there wasn't anything they could do about it. They told him to take it back and wait and see if another one comes." She went to a narrow rolltop desk in the front hall and opened the drawer. "I'm not supposed to talk about it in school," she said, but she handed Matt an envelope. "Promise you won't say anything."

Matt looked at the envelope. BERRINGER was written in block letters on the front. Stupid, he thought. They couldn't even spell the name right.

Inside was a single sheet of paper. He unfolded it and saw, as though he had expected it, words cut out of newspapers and magazines, glued to the paper to form a message. It was just the way they described it in the Hardy Boys mysteries. Only it was real. Someone had actually sat down and found the words, and cut and pasted them. And delivered it.

Matt smoothed the sheet and read it.

You and your kind don't belong here. Get out— and your wife and daughter, too. Before it's too late. We mean business.

He read it again. Hate seemed to leap right off the paper. He put it down quickly. It was awful to think about a person hating that much. And sneaky enough to express it that way. He felt his face getting red.

"My dad would never do anything like that," he said, feeling as though he were really on the wrong side now.

"I know. He couldn't. He's your father. But someone did. And I'm scared."

Matt tried to think how he could comfort her. "Maybe your father should, like, lay off for a while.

You know. Not talk about protesting or show movies or stuff . . . ."

"Forget it," Allie interrupted, sounding angry herself. "He'd never go back on something he believes. Even if it doesn't work, he says, at least you stood up for what you thought. Then it's part of history, even if it's just a 'little protest in a little town somewhere.' "

She looked at him fiercely, as if she dared him to disagree, when all he wanted was to be on her side. He wanted to say he'd protest with her. But the "little town somewhere" was Hancock, his town, and it was his football team, too, and it seemed as though he'd waited all his life to make it. He began to feel angry, too, as though she had made him defend himself. Maybe it *was* better to let grown-ups handle this stuff, he thought.

He knew he couldn't begin to explain all the different ways he was feeling. So he turned back to the book they'd been working on. He had read only two more pages, with Allie putting notes into the outline, when his mother drove up and walked toward the house.

Allie's parents came out on the porch to greet her. They chatted for a few minutes, the Behringers nodding toward the house, inviting her to come in. Matt saw her shake her head as he and Allie said good-bye. He wished they could all be friends and that there never was such a thing as a missile or a protest. Or that he had never gotten to like Allie so much. He didn't really wish that, though.

He was silent in the car.

"All right, Matt," his mother said. "I guess I can hold my curiosity about your visit for a while. Of course, it *was* a long drive. . . ."

"Sorry, Mom." He tried to tell her about the paintings and the goats and the books all over, but he felt as though he were telling secrets. It sounded grudging and flat, even to him.

"Another time," his mother said. "It's not easy when parents aren't friendly."

That's the least of it, he thought. He was silent again the rest of the way home, wishing he could be in two places at once on the Saturday of the protest. Still, the social studies report was going to be all right. And Allie liked him. He was sure of that.

Chapter Eight

BY Tuesday, everyone in town seemed to be talking about missiles. There was a story in that day's newspaper about the sit-in protest; the army said it would call out the National Guard if necessary to get the missiles through to the base.

"I told you," Matt's father said at dinner Tuesday night. "It's really going to be a mess. Behringer's going to wish he'd never heard of this town."

"But, Dad," Matt said, "I read the paper and it doesn't say anything about him. I mean, not his name or anything."

"I'm sorry, Matt. I know you like Allie, and she does sound like a nice kid. But kids don't know everything, and I'm telling you, Behringer's involved in this thing."

"Maybe he's nice, too," Matt's mother said. "Just doesn't happen to think the way you do."

"That's not fair," Mr. Tyson said. "You know I spoke up for him at the veterans' meeting. But I still think there's going to be trouble."

His father sounded like a sheriff telling everyone to take cover before the gunfight, Matt thought. He wished he could ask him how serious an anonymous letter might be, but he'd promised not to tell.

It was a hard week. He kept thinking about the letter, and how scared Allie seemed for her father. Matt knew *he* hadn't done anything wrong, but he still felt guilty.

In the hall after math, Matt found himself standing still, silent, and alone. Paul asked, "What's the matter? You're so quiet." Matt moved over to where Paul and Terry were dueling with the rulers they'd been using and grabbed one to get himself into the action. With the guys, that was easy. He tried to remember to keep alert, to join in the kidding around in the halls between classes and in the locker room before practice.

With Allie it was awful. She seemed to be there every time he turned around. When he was alone with her for a minute before study hall, he couldn't answer at all when she asked what was wrong. "Are you mad at me?" she asked.

"No," he said, "what would I be mad for?" But he still couldn't talk to her. Finally, she just went to sit with Mandy and the cheerleaders.

Paul had a different idea. "I know your problem," he said triumphantly, after Matt had been absolutely silent during one whole lunch period. "You're in love."

Terry overheard and joined in. "Lover boy!"

"Allie's got you going." Chris grabbed and hugged himself. Matt's face was scarlet as Paul began to hum the "Wedding March." He punched Matt's arm lightly.

Matt turned to punch Paul back and knocked his tray off the table. The clatter made other kids turn around to look, and he was glad he had to duck down to pick everything up.

Mr. Behringer gave them time during Thursday's social studies class to work on their reports. Matt was all right as long as he and Allie stuck to the Crusade. Several times, though, she turned to him with a questioning look.

Each time, he just turned back to the report and wrote some more, leaving Allie no choice but to do the same. They had nearly finished the report by the end of class.

"We can do the last section over the weekend," Allie said. "I can come to your house this time, if you want."

"I'm sorry," Matt said, feeling even worse. "I guess I didn't tell you. Me and my dad and Paul are going camping this weekend. You know, 'cause Monday is Columbus Day. We're leaving right after the game."

"Oh."

"I'm sorry," Matt said again. "I mean, I'm not sorry about camping. It's the best. I'm sorry we can't finish the report then."

"We're nearly done anyway," Allie said. "We still have time next week." She sounded so organized and cool. She wasn't even looking at him anymore.

"Hey, Allie." She stopped fussing with the papers. "I really like working with you."

She smiled and brushed back her hair, the way he liked her best. "I thought maybe you didn't or you were mad or something." He shook his head. "Or got sick from goat's milk," she added with a grin.

"No way," he said. "I know, I've been really weird all week. Like . . . like I feel like I'm being pulled in two directions, and . . ." He trailed off.

"You don't have to go to the protest for me," she said.

"I want to," Matt snapped. "That's the problem. I want to, and I want to play football, too."

"I know," Allie said, "but don't blame it on me." She looked angry now, and that made him feel even worse.

"Oh, Allie," was all he could get out. His pain must have shown because she smiled at him at last.

It made him feel a little better, even though nothing had changed.

PRACTICE that afternoon lasted a little longer than usual. Coach Wilson had them running more complicated plays now, and he let the seventh-graders practice more of the time to get ready for the game against Highland Falls. They were the worst team in the league, and Hancock always beat them by twenty or thirty points. It was a tradition to let the younger boys have their chance then.

As Matt walked out of the locker room and headed for the bike racks, he heard fire engines racing toward the school.

"Oh, wow," Terry yelled. "Maybe the whole school will burn and we won't have to do our reports."

Matt saw a plume of black smoke coming from the teachers' parking area. He started to run toward it, followed by Paul and Terry. As they got closer, he thought he could see a car burning. It looked orange, like the Behringers' little Volkswagen bug. His stomach felt tight at the thought. But maybe it was just the flames he was seeing. Two firemen stopped them before they could get any closer and told them to go home.

"It's just a trash fire, nothing to worry about. School as usual tomorrow, I'm afraid," one said.

The boys stood watching for a few minutes longer. Matt wondered how adults thought they could get away with such obvious lies.

"Maybe it'll be on the news tonight," Paul said.

Matt listened to the radio that night and watched the TV news, but there was nothing about the fire.

He tried to call Allie, but there was no answer. He felt almost relieved at first, but when he tried again at ten o'clock and there was still no answer, it scared him. Nobody stayed out that late on a week night in Hancock. Maybe it *was* trash burning, like the fireman had said, he told himself. But then, why was the smoke so black? Forget it, he thought, there's nothing you can do about it now.

THE next morning there was a substitute teacher in social studies, and Allie wasn't there either. "What's up?" Matt asked Terry.

"I'm not sure. I heard some teachers talking outside the principal's office. Something about Behringer's car being burned."

Matt looked at Terry hard, to make sure he wasn't teasing.

"It could be just a rumor," Terry said.

"Maybe," Matt said doubtfully.

The substitute was asking for them please to settle down and turn to page eighty-two. Her voice made it clear that it wasn't the first time she'd asked.

Matt got out his book but realized he couldn't just sit there. He felt for a quarter in his pocket. At least he could try to call. He went out the door as though he were going to the bathroom. He guessed he must really look bad because the teacher didn't say anything.

He dialed Allie's number and let the phone ring fifteen times before he hung up. He tried again. But it was the same—there was no answer.

He went back to class, finally, and tried to pay attention. He called again right before lunchtime. Still no answer. Midway through lunch, Mr. Harmon, the principal, came in and made an announcement.

"As many of you have heard, an automobile belonging to one of our teachers, Mr. Behringer, was set on fire and destroyed yesterday afternoon by unknown vandals. Fortunately, no one was hurt. But this kind of senseless violence cannot be tolerated. I hope that anyone who knows anything about this will feel free to come tell me about it. Are there any questions?" The principal's long, droopy face pulled itself into what tried to be a pleasant expression.

Of course, Mandy raised her hand.

"Yes, my dear."

"My father says this is one of the worst things that's ever happened in Hancock." She blushed and seemed ready to go on, but the principal interrupted.

"Thank you, Mandy. I know we all share his feeling." As he turned to leave, the lunchroom erupted into a hundred different conversations.

Matt, with the football team, didn't say anything. He hadn't touched his sandwich, and his hands were in tight fists on the table in front of him.

"You okay?" Paul asked.

"Sure." Matt tried to sound casual.

"I know what you're worried about, but Harmon did say no one was hurt."

Matt looked again at Paul. "But there wasn't any answer at their house when I tried to call last night or this morning." He got up. "I'm going to try again now."

Paul followed him. There was still no answer at the Behringers' house.

"Why would anyone burn his car?" Paul asked.

"It's got to have something to do with the missile protest. Allie even said she was worried." Matt would have liked to tell Paul about the anonymous letter, too. After all, if they wanted Mr. Behringer out of town bad enough . . . But Allie had said the letter was a secret.

THIS was the worst week he'd ever had, Matt thought, when the bell rang at the end of Friday. Football practice helped. You couldn't think of anything else at all while that was going on. But when he got home, he tried calling again. Still no answer.

After supper, he asked his mother if she'd drive him out to the Behringers' house. But she thought that wouldn't be right. "Maybe they're just not answering the phone, Matt. Maybe they don't want to be disturbed."

He didn't believe that. He had such an awful feeling that they were gone or dead or something, and he'd never see Allie again.

Without asking or telling anyone, knowing what answer he'd get, he went out the back door as quietly as he could, got out his bike, and started to ride the ten miles out to Allie's house. He had left a note on his door, so his parents wouldn't worry when they couldn't find him. And he'd put on his jacket that had a night-bright stripe on the back, so the cars could see him.

Even so it was scary, riding at night. The cars coming up behind him seemed to be going much too fast in the dark, and the blast of air behind them made the bike shake. By the time he'd ridden about halfway, he was on the back roads, and there were hardly any cars there. But it was dark and awfully quiet. He wished there *would* be another car, so he wouldn't be alone.

Then he did hear one. It was slowing up behind him, instead of breezing past, and he watched it pull over to the edge of the road just ahead of him. It was their van; his father got out. Matt rode up to him and stopped.

"You can't do this, Matt," his father said. "It's late. You have a game tomorrow. It's too dangerous to ride along this road at night."

"But I have to know if Allie's all right. I have to. I have to find out what happened." He started to ride away, but his father's hand shot out to grip the handlebars.

"I said no, Matt." Mr. Tyson's voice had an edge to it that told Matt he was getting really angry. But Matt felt desperate.

"Will you drive me there, then?"

"I thought you'd already discussed that with

Mom. They're probably staying somewhere else for a couple of days, that's all."

Matt felt put down. He hadn't thought of that. He wanted to fight back. "How do you know? Do you know who burned that car, too?" His voice came out sounding mad and defiant. He was afraid of the answer he'd get, afraid he was going too far.

"No, but I know they're all right. And I do think they're staying somewhere else for a while, till this blows over."

"How do you know?" Matt sounded whiny even to himself, but he couldn't help it.

"Matt, I'm your father. *I'm* telling you. People were talking about this all day today. I know, that's all. Now put your bike in the van and get in."

"You know the guys that did it, right?" He was scared as soon as he said it. It was almost like accusing his father.

"Matt, that's enough. Get in the car, I said." Now his father *was* angry. His voice had that cold sound that Matt had learned meant the end of his patience. Matt got off his bike, opened the van doors, and started to lift the bike in. His father was beside him, helping. Silently, they got into the front seat.

As they drove back to the house Matt could feel his father's anger. When they were almost there, Mr. Tyson spoke. "The answer to your question is no,

Matt. I don't know who did it, but I know who didn't. It wasn't my friends or anyone I know. They talk tough sometimes, but they're not sneaky. And guys who've been in a war don't think violence is for fun. You'd better believe it." They pulled into the driveway as he finished speaking. Matt didn't argue, but he wasn't sure he believed it either. He walked into the house. His mom was at the front door. He just walked past her, up to his room.

He got angrier the more he thought about the whole thing. He thought he'd like to go beat up whoever had done it. But it wasn't kids, and what could he do against grown-ups? Violent ones. And besides, then he'd be doing just what they were doing. He felt absolutely powerless, the way he used to in play fights, when his father could just stick his arm out and keep Matt's blows from landing at all.

He knew he should be getting his sleep for the football game in the morning. But he felt as though he couldn't until he'd figured out a way to show Allie, and even Mr. Behringer, that he was on their side.

There wasn't any good answer. But finally he knew what he had to do. The protest was on a football Saturday. Allie understood how important that was. Well, never mind. He'd give up that game for the protest, if he had to, and hope to make the team again next year. He'd be on Allie's side that morning, and maybe that would make a difference. He socked his fist into his open hand. He felt better having made up his mind. He still couldn't fall asleep, though.

He switched on the radio, so he'd have something to listen to besides what was in his own head. It didn't solve the problem, but as he lay back and half-listened, he began to think there might be a way to convince even Paul that he was right.

Finally, he fell asleep.

Chapter Nine

THE next morning Paul came to Matt's house early to drop off his sleeping bag and knapsack for the camping trip. "I think I've got everything your dad told me to bring," Paul said. "And you said you had an extra pair of those boots to wear when we're fishing?"

"Yeah, they're my dad's old ones. He got new ones this year. And mine from last year still fit."

"Do you think we'll really catch a lot, big enough to eat, I mean?"

"We always do," Matt answered, trying to sound cool and experienced. But he had awakened feeling excited. He remembered the smell of the fire and the hot pan and the fish frying. Nothing else tasted as good. His father always did it just right. Matt wasn't mad at him anymore.

They walked back to the garage. Paul dumped his things in the van, Matt got his bike, and they rode off to the game. It was getting to be routine now, and there was no big send-off as there had been the first time. But his father's rabbit's foot stayed tucked in Matt's sock for luck, and he was glad that his parents would be there watching, as always, when the game began.

He wished Allie would be there, too, so he could stop worrying about her. But she wasn't. He forced himself to stop thinking about the Behringers and concentrate on the game.

In the second half, again when the team was ahead, Coach Wilson gave him a chance. On the first couple of plays he was just a decoy. Once Bobby Harneman faked a handoff to him on a reverse and ran with the ball. Then Harneman passed to Jim, while Matt ran down the other side to draw some of the defenders. On the third play, Bobby threw to him, and Matt just managed to get his fingers on the ball and pull it in before he was tackled, hard. He got up slowly, bent over a little, trying to get his breath back. As he reached the huddle, he saw that Coach Wilson had sent in some subs. Even Bobby was leaving—and Paul was there! Matt knew it wasn't cool, but he put his arm around Paul and gave him a hug anyway.

On the first play, Paul faded back and threw to Ken Akers. Matt thought he looked nervous, and the pass hit the ground in front of Ken as he turned to reach for it. Paul tried a running play next, handing off to Jim for a five-yard gain.

Now it was third down, and Matt watched Paul trying to decide what to do. He knew Paul should probably hand off again, but he would naturally want to try another pass.

He did. "Matt, you and Jim both go out for the pass," he said in the huddle.

Matt saw the pass coming for him. It was much too low, but he had to get it. He dove and just managed to hold on as he skidded and tumbled over the grass.

"Thanks, Matt," Paul said. It was first down again, and Paul sounded more sure of himself. But on the next pass, intended for Ken, he waited too long to throw, and the pass was intercepted.

"I messed up again," he said, disgusted with himself, walking back to the bench as the defensive team came in.

"Oh, c'mon, Paul," Matt said. "Every quarterback gets intercepted. Anyway, you got good distance on the pass you threw to me."

"Yeah, and you made a miracle catch to save it."
Paul shook his head. "And now I gave it away. I should have thrown to you again. It works when I do."

"Okay, so you will next time. I'll try to get free."

"If there is a next time."

Matt looked at Paul sitting there, with his head down. Why is it that when I need to talk the most, he thought, I can never think of what to say?

AFTER the game, they piled into the Tysons' van, crammed with backpacks, sleeping bags, fishing gear, and food. The tent and the canoe were lashed down on the roof carrier, and the fishing rods, carefully disassembled and in their cases, lay across the shelf behind the backseat.

They drove northwest into the mountains, and then along Matt's favorite road that ran, like the grand avenue of a palace, between borders of tall pines. Finally, they went off onto the dirt road that led to the stream. They had just enough time to set up the tent and collect firewood before it was dark. Mr. Tyson heated some stew that Matt's mom had made for them the night before. While Matt and Paul carried water from the stream for coffee and got out the bowls and forks, he filled the two lanterns with kerosene. After supper, they got sticks to roast marshmallows over the embers of the fire.

This was when Matt really loved to listen to his dad tell stories about when he was a kid, camping with a friend. The best one was about the time a bear had visited their tent, terrifying them, batting at the outside with its paws while they scrunched down inside their sleeping bags. Finally, one of the boys had gotten brave enough to take the food bag and quickly throw it out the tent flap, as far as he could. The bear raised its head, followed the sound, and padded away with the bag, never to return.

"We didn't get much sleep that night," Mr. Tyson laughed. "But at least we learned never to keep food inside a tent."

"Tell about the time you went up the other fork of the stream and nearly got sucked into the waterfall," Matt said. He loved the feeling of sitting with the fire warm in front of them and the dark, black night beginning right at their backs.

"I'll tell that one tomorrow," his father said. "But I want you guys up early tomorrow, building the fire for breakfast. Paul's just about asleep anyway."

Matt looked at Paul, head on his knees, sort of snuffling as he breathed. Very quietly, so as not to wake him, Matt asked, "Then please just tell about when you were in the war, and you went after the guy who was wounded and your leg was hurt."

His father looked at Matt, smiled a little sadly, and nodded.

Matt had heard the story several times by now, but he still found himself almost holding his breath when his father told about going back for his friend.

"I had been hit in the arm by that time, but I didn't even feel it. I knew I had to get Pete out of there, or he'd die for sure. I asked one of the other guys to watch for snipers, and I started crawling out into the open again. I got to Pete, all right, and I'd pulled him almost all the way back, when I heard something like a big thump, deep in the jungle on the other side of the clearing. I stopped moving for a second. I guess that was my mistake. Anyway, the next thing I heard was a mortar shell hitting the ground, right behind me. And that was all I knew till I woke up in the hospital."

Matt moved closer to his father and leaned against him. He asked the same question he'd asked the last time he'd heard the story. "How could you not be too scared to do it? How could you be so brave?"

And again, his father said, "We were scared, all right. We were out there alone, and we figured we were going to die. But you don't think about what you're doing. You just do it."

They were both quiet for a minute, watching the fire.

"And then you woke up in the hospital. And your lcg—"

"Enough for now." He put his arm around Matt's shoulder and kissed the top of his head. He spoke a little louder. "Get yourselves to bed now."

Paul jerked his head up and mumbled, "Just staring at the fire." Both boys got up and went into the tent. They took off only their jackets and shoes and slipped into their sleeping bags.

THE morning fishing was good. Matt's father was a patient teacher, helping them to cast again and again till the fly landed just right. He showed them where to find the quiet pools that might hold hungry fish. Matt already knew how to clean and scale the ones they caught. His father expected him to do that for himself now. But he showed Paul how, and got a Band-Aid from the emergency kit when Paul cut himself.

After lunch, while Mr. Tyson fished some more, Matt and Paul went up the stream in the other direction to count the number of small waterfalls it took for the stream to get down from its route between the foothills of the mountain. By the fifteenth, they were ready to take off their sneakers and dangle their feet in the small pool under the falls.

It was easy to forget about the tent and sleeping

114

bags and fishing equipment, and feel as though they were on their own there, in the wilderness. Matt loved that. It was a way of understanding what it was like to be part of nature, without a name or a family or a school.

Paul finally spoke, breaking the mood. "Do you think Coach Wilson will let the seventh-graders play most of the game next week? You know, the way he always does against Highland Falls?"

Matt was startled; he'd been thinking that game was the following week. He didn't answer right away.

Paul was insistent. "What do you think? I mean, even if I messed up yesterday, I could get another chance." When Matt still didn't say anything, Paul went on. "And then I could pass to you, and I wouldn't be so nervous."

Matt pulled his feet out of the water and stood up. He hadn't wanted to talk about it so soon. He'd wanted the camping trip to be perfect.

"What's the matter?" Paul asked.

There was no way around it. "I'm not going to play next Saturday," Matt said.

"What do you mean you're not going to play? You and Terry are the seventh-grade stars. I bet you'll play the whole game."

"That's not what I mean." He took a deep breath. "I'm going to be in that protest Saturday morning."

Paul got up fast, splashing them both. He stood opposite Matt, his face getting red. He opened his mouth and closed it again. "You can't do that, idiot! Coach Wilson will kick you right off the team if you miss a game."

"Then I'll play next year."

"You're crazy!" Paul put his hands on Matt's shoulders and shook him, as if Matt were a child having a tantrum.

Matt pulled away. "Maybe. But I have to do it. I have to stand up for what I think." He paused for a few seconds. "Besides, I've got to help Allie." He was sorry the minute he said it.

"Oh, I get it," Paul said angrily. "You love Allie, Allie's going to protest, so you're going, too. Never mind football, and the fact that we practiced for years to make this team. You're so good you'll make the team next year anyway. Never mind that I'm *never* going to look good if I can't pass to you."

Matt felt as though Paul's words were rocks falling on his head. Paul was right, and it hurt.

"Listen," Matt said urgently. "It isn't only Allie. It's me. You know I didn't like those missiles from the beginning. I don't want them around here. If anything happens, I don't want us to be nuked. I don't want anybody to be nuked."

"Oh, c'mon, Matt, nobody's going to get nuked. There's not going to be any war, and anyway, who's

116

going to care if one more twelve-year-old marches in some dumb protest."

Matt didn't say anything. That made Paul even madder. "You've got to admit it, you're just being stupid."

Matt thought back to the first time they'd seen the missile. "When we first saw that thing, you didn't like it either. I thought maybe you'd go with us."

"Sure I would, if it wasn't on a football morning," Paul said. "I'm telling you, nobody's going to care if a million kids go, so why do *you* have to? It's not going to make any difference."

"Maybe not," Matt said, beginning to get angry, "but sometimes kids do make a difference. Anyway, it makes a difference to me."

"Great," Paul answered sarcastically. "So you sacrifice me, and the team maybe, for some dumb idea and a girl!"

They weren't getting anywhere. Matt bent over and pulled his socks on, tugging and stretching them where his feet were still wet. He shoved his feet into his sneakers, tied them quickly, and started down the side of the stream back to the campsite.

He had been thinking so much about his own loss if he didn't play in the game, he hadn't really thought about anybody else's. He had figured Paul would just go on and play. And the team would go on to win no matter what. "I'm the only one who's

117

really losing anything," he muttered, half-aloud. He had gotten as far as the next waterfall when he heard Paul shout.

"Hey, wait for me. I'm coming back, too."

Matt stopped and waited, watching the bugs skitter across the surface of the water. He couldn't see any fish. Paul came hurrying down the side of the stream, crunching the leaves and twigs. Matt had forgotten how easily Paul felt spooked in the woods, how much he didn't like to be alone here. He thought about how long they had been best friends, about trying one more time to make Paul understand. But he knew he didn't really understand all his own feelings himself.

They walked back to the campsite, one behind the other, without speaking. Collecting firewood, building the fire, shoving potatoes into the coals to bake, Matt and Paul were so quiet that Matt's father finally noticed.

"What's got into you two? Worn out?" he asked. "Maybe we'd all better get to sleep early. I thought we'd have time to drive down to the river tomorrow morning and do a little white-water canoeing before we have to go home."

"Oh, wow," Matt said, smiling for the first time since that morning.

Paul looked a little bit doubtful. Matt knew it was something he'd never done before.

In the tent, just before they fell asleep, Matt said, "You can trust my dad. His leg doesn't matter. He really knows what he's doing on the water. It'll be fun." He wanted Paul not to be scared, to go to sleep looking forward to the speedy, splashy ride.

ALTHOUGH they had their own canoe, they stopped at the place where you could rent them to go down the river. Mr. Tyson explained that he would ask the son of the owner to drive down and meet them at the end of the rapids. That way, they could take the canoe back to the starting place on his truck and go down again.

The first time down the rapids, Mr. Tyson took Paul. Then he took Matt. He made them wear life jackets and told them how to look for rocks coming up under the water by watching the patterns in the current. He showed them how to fend them off with the canoe paddles. "Just don't panic," he said. "The worst that can happen is that you go overboard, and then all you have to do is ride it out, feet first, so you don't hit a rock with your head."

After each ride, they pulled the canoe out and portaged it up the bank to the road where the truck was waiting. When Matt and Paul had each gone twice, Matt begged to be allowed to try it alone.

"Not yet," Mr. Tyson said. "I just don't think you're strong enough."

"Please, Dad."

"Well . . . why don't you and Paul go together. I think you can handle that now."

"Want to?" Matt turned to Paul, who looked a little uncertain, but said yes.

Mr. Tyson told them again how to watch for the hidden rocks.

"We'll be okay, Dad. I promise."

Everything was fine till about three-quarters of the way down the rapids. Paul relaxed and started yelling like a cowboy as they went through the wildest current. Then, somehow, he got his paddle stuck between a rock and a jammed log and lost it. Reaching out to get it, he leaned too far and suddenly went overboard, holding on to the edge of the canoe and pulling it over with him.

Matt splashed into the water, caught his breath, and tried to get his feet facing forward as his father had told him. He was still holding on to his paddle.

He could hear Paul yelling for help, a little way ahead of him, and tried to steer himself over that way. He watched the canoe slide by, half-underwater, but he couldn't catch it.

Paul yelled again, jammed against a rock. Matt came alongside him, moving fast. He managed to grab Paul's life jacket for a moment, but the current was too strong for him to hold on.

Then Matt heard his father yell from the river-bank, "Take care of yourself, Matt. I'll get Paul."

He tried to turn for a second to see what was happening, but he was carried downstream. He knew his father was a terrific swimmer. "Water makes me equal again," he had often said. But Matt didn't know how the artificial leg would work in the swift current or against the rocks underneath.

As soon as he got to the quiet calm at the end of the rapids, he turned and looked back. His father, holding Paul by his life jacket, was coming up beside him. There was no sign of the canoe.

They swam to shore and scrambled up the bank, Matt automatically reaching his hand out for his father to pull on, while he stood up on his good leg. But nothing had stopped his dad from rescuing Paul.

Mr. Tyson looked at the boys and shook his head. "Are you guys okay?" he asked. "Either of you hurt?"

Matt just grinned and shook his head. He felt terrific, in fact. Paul shook his head, too, but he stood there shivering and looking miserable, even though the air was Indian-summer warm.

"Let's get back and get some dry clothes," Mr. Tyson said. "Then we can try to get what's left of the canoe. I saw it, caught on a log, near the bank a little way back." He turned to look at both boys. "What happened?"

"We were going down just perfectly," Matt started, "and then Paul's paddle got stuck between a rock and a log—"

"It wasn't my fault," Paul interrupted. "Matt got us turned halfway around, and I was afraid we were going to get swamped."

"I didn't say it was your fault," Matt said hotly. "I just said your paddle got stuck."

Paul glared at him but said nothing.

"Anyway," Matt went on, "when you grabbed for it, you went over, and the canoe went over, too."

"Yeah," Paul said, "because you were leaning out the same way."

"So it's my fault? Bull! You just panicked."

"Liar!"

Matt moved without thinking. The next thing he knew, he was on top of Paul, trying to wrestle him down, and Paul was hitting him wherever the life jacket wasn't protecting him. They fell to the ground. Their wet clothes slipped on the leaves, and they rolled toward the water, grunting and trying to hit each other.

"Cut it out," Matt's father yelled, grabbing Matt and pulling him away from Paul.

Hearing the noise, the owner's son had gotten out of the truck and now helped Paul to his feet. He held him there, away from Matt.

"What's the matter with you?" Mr. Tyson asked. "Matt, you come in the back of the truck with me. Paul can sit inside with the driver."

Matt watched his father boost himself up onto the back of the truck with his good leg, and then pull himself along till he was sitting with his back up against the side. His arms were amazingly strong. He thought of his father jumping in to get Paul without thinking of his leg or anything.

Back at the campsite Matt and Paul were sent into the tent to change, one by one, so they couldn't fight again. Like when we were in kindergarten, Matt thought, calm now.

Mr. Tyson was packing things into the van. In their dry clothes, Matt and Paul took over while he changed. They still weren't talking. When they were all ready to go, Matt finally said, "I'm sorry about the canoe, Dad. I guess it really was my fault."

"You don't talk about fault with a thing like this," his father said kindly. "Accidents happen. Then you try to fix things. That's all."

"Can it be fixed?" Paul asked. "I'll pay for my share of it."

"We'll see when we get to where it is and take a good look at it. And we'll worry about the paying later." Mr. Tyson smiled. "I'm just glad the canoe got it, not either of you. You guys did pretty well, you know."

Matt felt all mixed up. He knew that he and Paul weren't just fighting about the canoe. It was really about missiles and football and maybe Allie, too. He thought his dad would surely be angry if he knew.

His father was saying something else, though, looking at him expectantly. "Hey, Matt? I said shake hands, and let's get going."

Matt stuck his hand out automatically, not really looking at Paul. Paul did the same, and they shook. Then they sat silently all the way home.

Chapter Ten

ON Tuesday, Matt woke up early and couldn't get back to sleep. He kept thinking of how angry the rest of the team was going to be, too. He would need Paul more than ever, and now he wasn't even sure his friend would come by for him this morning, though they'd fought and made up hundreds of times before.

After breakfast, he waited outside on his bike for Paul. Just as he checked his watch for the last time and started for the corner, Paul rode up behind him and bumped his back tire.

"Hi," Matt said over his shoulder, with a wide smile, happily bumping back.

He held his breath going upstairs to social studies

and didn't let it out till he saw Mr. Behringer and Allie. To his enormous relief, they looked the same as always. That was all he'd been hoping for.

The class was very quiet, knowing that Mr. Behringer would say something about what had happened.

"You all know about the incident last week. I want you to know, besides, that I'm back because I like and respect you all, and I like living in this town." He paused and looked around the room. "In any town, though, when there's disagreement about something, there are always a few people who won't fight openly but would rather do something sneaky. Basically, that's what happened."

He moved around in front of his desk and sat on the edge of it. "Judging from the way you carry on in class, though, you guys are all *very* open in your disagreements." He smiled, and a few kids laughed obediently. "There may be some more trouble on Saturday, when the missiles are trucked in. But I think that will all be out in the open, and that's the way it should be."

He stood up again and began to talk about their Middle Ages reports, which were due Friday. He told them he'd let them have a work period in class on Thursday for any last-minute help they needed. Matt wished they'd have a work period right then, so he could talk to Allie.

"I'm glad you're back," he told her after class.

She smiled. "Me, too. We went down to New York and stayed with friends."

"That's what my dad said you'd do, but I wasn't sure."

"Nothing's changed, though," Allie said, her smile fading. "We're still going to the protest."

"So am I," Matt said quickly. "That's what I decided."

"But the game—"

Matt nodded. "I know. But it's what I want to do."

At lunchtime, he stopped to talk to her again for a minute before he went to the football table. When he got there, the others just glared at him as he sat down. Obviously Paul had told them about Matt's plan. No one said anything for a minute. And then they were all on him.

"You sure are some kind of a nut," Chris said. "This isn't for real."

"You're letting the seventh grade down," Tom said bitterly. "For what? You say that dumb protest. I say that girl." He sounded as though *girl* meant spider or scorpion. Matt felt his face getting red.

Terry refused to believe he wouldn't play. "You're kidding, right, testing us out or something?" Matt shook his head, and they started in again.

Suddenly he realized he wouldn't be able to sit there with the team now. He tried to take a bite of his sandwich, but couldn't eat. He got up and walked out of the lunchroom and sat on the steps outside.

The only thing left was to tell Coach Wilson. He didn't think he was strong enough to stand up to him and say it right out.

Allie came out and sat beside him.

"Aren't those supposed to be your friends? Looks like they were pretty rough."

"It isn't their fault," he said. "I made it happen. I can't be two places at once."

"I'm really sorry, Matt," she said, almost whispering. "I'm so sorry I got you into this."

He had to say, "I believe you." He did.

He took out his notebook to write a note to the coach. First he tried explaining how he felt about the missiles and how he had to protest. Then he tried to think of an excuse to let him out of just one game, but he knew his parents wouldn't back him up in a lie, and certainly not about this.

After he had crumpled up the first three starts, Allie, who had been trying not to look over his shoulder, said, "Matt, why don't you just go tell him?"

"I know," he said bitterly. "That's what your father would do. But you don't know Coach Wilson. I can't do it."

"What if you just don't show up Saturday?"

"I thought of that, too."

He took out another sheet of paper. "Dear Coach Wilson," he began, for the fourth time. "I can't play in the football game this Saturday. There is something else I have to do. I know the rules, but I hope you will let me play for you again someday. Sincerely, Matt Tyson."

He rubbed his eyes, folded the paper, and went inside to put it into the coach's mailbox. He stood there for a minute after he'd shoved the paper in, as if he might take it back, then turned and went up the stairs to math class with Allie. All afternoon he kept feeling as though Coach Wilson was going to reach out and grab him to make him say he'd play after all. He didn't go to practice, and when he got home early, his mom wanted to know if he was sick.

She and Dad have to know the truth sometime, he thought. So he told her.

"I wondered if you were still thinking about the protest," she said. "Then, when you didn't say anything more, I figured you'd forgotten about it." She looked over at his downcast face. "It must have been awful telling Paul and the guys."

He nodded.

"Dad doesn't know yet?"

"No." He must have looked as scared as he felt because his mother reached over and rumpled his hair.

"He may be mad for a bit. But he'll get over it. He loves you, you know. And I think you're terrific."

He shrugged, leaned his head against her for a moment, and then pulled away again. "It's just that Dad practiced so much with me, and he'll say he was counting on me. Like everyone else said."

In the end, his father said that and a lot more. He was angry and he let Matt know it.

"Look, Matt," he said. "I might understand if you'd been thinking about this for a long time, like football. I don't like you suddenly getting involved in these grown-up things without really knowing about them. They should leave you kids out of it."

Matt wished with all his heart they had, but he couldn't let his father make him back down now. "Dad," he said, "I'm old enough. I'll take the consequences." But that wasn't what his father was thinking about.

"Don't you appreciate living here where you *can* be a kid for a while and let football be important while the time's right?" he asked. He turned Matt's face toward him. "It's not for *me*," he said. "I played. I had my chance. I want it for you. That's something to fight for."

Matt felt his throat tighten. He fought to keep control. "You can't stop me."

"All right!" Mr. Tyson shouted. "But if anything happens, you're on your own. Don't expect me to come and bail you out."

"Don't worry. I know I'm on my own." It was a lonely feeling.

THERE was no getting away from the subject of the protest. The local television station had begun to have stories about the nuclear missiles coming to the army base on Saturday, and the planned sit-in, and the National Guard being called out if necessary.

Wherever he went, Matt felt as though everyone was looking at him and being mad at him. The only time he felt a little better was on Wednesday night, when he went with Allie and her father to the final meeting for the protesters. Allie's mother wasn't there. She said she got too scared to be useful in a protest. But she had made lots of signs.

Matt had told his parents that he was going to Allie's house after school to finish their report and that Mr. Behringer would drive him home because he had to come back into town for a meeting. It was all true, except that Matt didn't tell them he was going to the meeting, too.

Matt knew a few of the people there. A man and woman Matt had never seen before seemed to be in charge. His mother's friend Jan, the other nursery-school teacher, was there, and another teacher from the middle school, and—to his astonishment—even Mandy's father, the mayor. "I'm not here because I'm going to protest," he said to them all. "It's just my duty to see that everything stays peaceful, so I have to know what's going on."

They showed slide pictures of the World War II bombings again to remind people of why they were protesting. "Missiles like the ones they want to put here are supposed to be so accurate that they can guarantee within half a mile where they will land," the woman leader told the group. "But let me ask you all, what would happen if a missile landed half a mile from this army base?"

Matt thought about that. The school was only half a mile on the other side.

Matt sat close to Allie and listened while the leaders went on telling people where they'd all meet, and how to sit down in a tight group right in front of the gates to the base, and how to relax their arm and leg muscles to make themselves heavy and limp when the police came to drag them away.

"We're probably not going to be able to stop the missiles from getting to the base," the woman leader said. "But we'll let people all over the country know what we think."

"And we'll keep the police busy, and the National

Guard, too, if it comes to that. They'll need to work hard getting all of us to jail," the other leader added.

Jail, Matt thought. He felt as though someone had punched him. He'd never really believed they meant that for kids, too. But he didn't want to seem scared, so he kept his mouth shut.

THE next day, with their report all finished, Matt and Allie made a cover during the work period. THE CHILDREN'S CRUSADE, Allie wrote in neat block letters. Matt drew a picture of hundreds of tiny figures, some carrying banners, marching over a hill toward the sea. "They did make some difference, I guess," he said. "At least people remember them." He looked questioningly at Allie, thinking about Saturday.

Allie nodded and wrote *by Allison Behringer and Matt Tyson,* in her best script, down at the bottom of the cover.

THEN, finally, it was Saturday. Allie was waiting at the end of Matt's driveway. They stood together for a moment, then joined the line of people starting to walk toward the edge of town. They could hear the soft sound of singing: "All we are saying is give peace a chance. . . ."

"Are you scared?" Matt asked.

"A little," Allie admitted. "My dad said, Please don't get arrested. Do you really think we might? That man talked about jail at the meeting."

"I don't think he meant for kids," Matt said. "I don't think they arrest kids." He wished he felt more sure.

"My dad said I could stand it—but he'd rather have it happen to him, if it has to happen at all. He's marching with the other teachers."

"But he didn't try to stop you?"

"Oh, no. He said I have to do what I think is right, just the way he does."

Matt thought about how he'd snuck out of the house this morning. He'd dressed, all but his shoes, and quietly slipped downstairs, walking on the edge of each step close to the wall so the stairs wouldn't squeak. At the last minute he'd taken the rabbit's foot from his dresser and put it in his pocket.

They were beginning to move toward the army base. You couldn't really call it marching, Matt thought. It was too ragged and casual for that. But they were certainly going to get there. There must have been two hundred of them, many of them people Matt and Allie hadn't seen before who had come from farther away to join the protest. Allie looked to see whether any other kids from the middle school were there. Matt had thought Tim might come, but he didn't see him. There were a few unfamiliar children, mostly younger, holding their mothers' hands and looking around.

As they marched out of town, nobody seemed to be paying any attention to them, though Allie nudged Matt to show him people looking out from behind their curtains. It felt strange to be looked at that way. Singing helped, and they were getting pretty loud as they came to the top of the hill before the base. Matt looked down over the marchers, with their signs. They looked small and indistinct, like the figures in the picture he'd drawn for the cover of their Crusade report.

They didn't hear the hecklers right away. Then, as they came around the last curve in the road, they saw a crowd lined up across from the main gate of the base, almost all men and older boys. Matt knew some of them from years of Little League. But they didn't look like fathers and older brothers now. They looked angry and mean. They were standing behind a line of state police wearing helmets and carrying clubs. The helmets had something funny on top of them.

Allie reached out for Matt's hand. "What's that on top of the cops' heads?" she asked. It took Matt a few minutes to figure out that they must be gas masks. He didn't say so.

"Gas masks," Allie whispered, when she realized. "That means they've got tear gas." Matt just nodded and frowned. He was looking again at the group of men behind the police. There was a man in a jacket just like his dad's. And then he realized that it *was* his father. Them against us, Matt thought.

"It's crazy, Allie," he said. "I thought we were just going to have a peaceful little sit-in, with some singing. Just to let them know how we felt."

"I know," she said. "This looks more like a war."

As the first group of people sat down in front of the gate to the base, three trucks roared up from the other direction and stopped abruptly.

"National Guard soldiers," Allie hissed. "Ooh, they've got guns." She shivered.

Now two huge flatbed trucks, each carrying a missile like the one Matt and Paul had first seen, lumbered up the final hill and stopped. Two soldiers picked their way around the men and women sitting in front of the gate and tried to swing it open. The people made it impossible, and they refused to move.

When the soldiers started to pull the protesters away, they went limp, as they had practiced doing, letting themselves be dragged, under arrest, to the waiting trucks. It took two men to move each person. As the first group of people were being dragged away, more moved in, to take their places. Again, two more guards pulled each of them away. Some men had driven up in a van, unloaded TV equipment, and were filming the scene.

Across the road, the men from town were shouting angrily. One of them broke through the line of police and grabbed a woman whose baby was in a carrier on her back.

"Go home," he shouted. "Go change your baby's diaper. You both stink." Quickly a policeman moved between them, and the woman, obviously scared, moved back into the crowd of marchers.

Allie looked at Matt, put her finger on her lips, and said, "Listen."

The men standing across the road were chanting something now:

"Nuke 'em till they go,
Nuke 'em till they glow."

Matt turned to Allie. "I can't believe they said that, ordinary people, people from here."

He looked at them hard. They probably *would* nuke us right now, if they had the weapons, he thought. That's the trouble. We're not even in a war and *that*'s what they're saying. He felt cold and wiggled his shoulders to get the creepy feeling away.

The whole group of marchers had reached the gate now, and they all sat down in the road, completely blocking the entrance to the base. Matt saw Mr. Behringer sitting near the gate.

One of the National Guardsmen spoke into a bullhorn. "Protesters, listen *now*. We have tear gas, and we will use it unless you disperse in the next sixty seconds. Please leave quietly. Tear gas is not pleasant."

He sounds so reasonable, Matt thought. As if we'd obey as a matter of course.

"Ten, nine, eight, seven, six, five, four, three, two, one, zero," the guardsman with the bullhorn counted. A few of the women with small children stood up and moved back across the road, away from the gate.

The sound of the tear-gas canister being shot off was like a small explosion. It only took a few seconds for Matt's eyes to start stinging and his nose to be running. It did feel like tears, he thought, but he wasn't crying.

Coughing, he looked for Allie in the smoky haze. He couldn't see her. Just people running in all directions. Even most of the men who had been shouting at them had pulled back down the road as the gas spread. Matt couldn't see whether his father was still there. His eyes were running, and he began to feel sick to his stomach. Police and soldiers grabbed people and dragged them to the trucks.

Suddenly he saw that one of them was Allie. He started to run, dodging past women and children and policemen, blocking everything else out, the way he had run downfield in his first football game. He hurled himself at the soldier who held Allie, butting his head into the man's stomach. Allie pulled loose as the man stumbled.

"Run," Matt shouted, "run for it!" He held on around the soldier's legs as he fell himself. In a moment, the soldier was on top of him, his knee against Matt's back. Matt tried to slide out from under him, but the man was strong and very angry.

"You're not getting out of this one, you little Commie rat," he said.

Matt lay still, getting his breath back. The soldier's knee was still heavy on his back. Matt concentrated for a minute, then tried to twist free by curling up suddenly. He got halfway up, but the man reached out and caught Matt's ankle, bringing him down again.

Matt felt his wrist being forced back against his arm as he fell. It hurt enough to make him helpless for a minute, and he lay still. The man rose up over him, swearing quietly and steadily, and started to drag Matt by his feet to the waiting trucks.

Most of the tear gas was gone, but Matt's eyes were still full of tears, this time from pain and anger. He felt furious and helpless being dragged, but the man's hands were so tight and strong there was no chance of getting away. Besides, Matt thought, this is what we were supposed to do. Make them drag us away.

His head bumped against the ground unless he really worked at holding it up, and his wrist hurt a lot. It was almost a relief to get inside the truck. One of the women who had been at the meeting was sitting quietly inside.

"Are you okay?" she asked. She sounded tender, the way his mom did when he came home hurt. But he didn't want to be treated like a kid now.

"I'm all right," he said, "just a little scratched up." He couldn't help looking at his wrist, just to see. It was already getting swollen.

Two more people were pushed into the truck, with tears streaming down their faces. A woman holding a little boy was next. He was crying quietly and steadily, not making much noise.

Matt edged over beside him. "It was scary, wasn't it?" he said.

The little boy nodded, still crying. "We're safe in here, though," Matt said. He tried to think of something to distract him and remembered the rabbit's foot he'd put in his pocket that morning. If it was lucky for football, he'd thought, maybe it would be lucky for a sit-in. Maybe not, Matt thought now.

"Here," he said. "Do you know what this is?"

The boy shook his head but looked intently into Matt's hand.

"It's my lucky rabbit's foot. Want to hold it?"

The little boy took it, felt the softness, and rubbed it against his cheek. He put his thumb in his mouth and stopped crying. His mother looked at Matt gratefully.

The truck filled up. The last one in was Jan, his mother's friend. She looked around and saw Matt as the truck began to move.

"Oh, Matt," she said. "They caught you, too."

Everyone in the truck looked tired, and they were all red-eyed from the tear gas. Another small child had vomited on his clothes, and the truck smelled awful. It was a relief when they rolled to a stop and a policeman let them out. They were in front of the police station, in the middle of town.

They really are going to put us in jail, Matt thought. They were half-led, half-pushed into the police station. Someone was taking their fingerprints and asking their names. When it was Matt's turn, he held out his left hand. He didn't want anyone touching his right wrist. It had really begun to hurt.

"Right hand, sonny," the policeman said. Matt raised his right arm a little to show him.

"That looks kind of bad," the policeman said. "Maybe we can get a doctor to check it later." He didn't sound mean, Matt thought, but he didn't really sound as though he cared either. He held Matt's left hand on the ink pad, then pressed each fingertip down on a card. "Name and address," he said. Matt told him and then was led down the hall to one of the town's two jail cells. They were already so full that everyone was sitting on the tile floor.

Matt sat down between Jan and the little boy who had been in the truck with him. He looked at his wrist. It was beginning to turn blue in places, and he could hardly move it at all now. He felt sick again when he looked at it. Even if Coach Wilson doesn't kick me off the team, I won't be playing for a while, he thought. He suddenly wondered how Paul had done in the game.

He held his right arm up against his chest. It felt better that way. He felt cold. The cell began to get dark as the sun went down. The door swung open and bright lights were turned on.

Several of the women stood up to post bail money so they could be released. Jan's husband came for her. She pointed out Matt, sitting there, and tried to get the police to release him, too. Her husband argued with the police chief, who said he could only release Matt to the custody of his own family or a lawyer. Finally, they gave up, wished Matt luck, and went away.

Matt wished his father would come for him, but he knew both of them had meant what they'd said.

He felt terribly alone, although there were still a few other people there.

At six o'clock, one of the policemen brought sandwiches and sodas. Matt picked up a sandwich and put it down again. He drank a little bit of soda, but even that made him feel sick.

Another hour passed. He and the woman with the little boy were the only ones left.

Someone had given the little boy a lollipop. He walked over to Matt and poked him on the cheek with it, offering him a lick. Matt tried to smile at him and just shook his head. Then the boy took the rabbit's foot, sticky now, and rubbed it gently on Matt's face. "All better now," he said, and went back to sit on his mother's lap. When Matt looked over at him again, after a few minutes, he had fallen asleep.

For just a minute, Matt wished he were little and asleep somewhere. He closed his eyes, but he didn't feel sleepy.

The cell door opened again for the little boy's father. He picked up his son and put his arm around his wife, kissed her, and started to lead her out of the cell.

"Good luck, Matt," she said. "Good-bye."

The police chief stood at the door of the cell. "Are you sure you don't want to make a telephone call, son?" he asked Matt, for the third time. He had explained Matt's rights to him, but Matt couldn't see what difference a call would make. He had agreed he'd be on his own.

He was proud of himself for not trying to go back on his word and call home, not trying to make the police feel sorry for him like a kid, even when his wrist hurt the most. But he also felt as though he might be there forever, the way he remembered feeling when his mother had come late to pick him up after school, and he was the last one left.

It was very quiet now, and getting colder. His jacket had felt warm when he'd left home that morning, but he was freezing now.

He heard the door to the station slam, and a voice he knew. "Dad," he called. His voice sounded hoarse. He got up slowly, feeling stiff. The cell door opened, and there was his father.

He hugged Matt carefully, seeing the wrist. "Can you walk all right?" he asked. Matt nodded. His throat felt so tight he couldn't say anything. He started walking slowly toward the door, concentrating on breathing in and out, so he wouldn't cry. His father came up beside him.

"Aren't you mad?" Matt asked softly as they got into the van. "I saw you there today, with all those guys yelling at us."

His father took a deep breath. "I saw you there,

too, Matt. I wasn't yelling, but I was good and mad. Then I saw you tackle that policeman to let Allie get away." He paused for a minute and turned to look at Matt in the seat beside him. "You weren't going to leave your buddy in enemy hands, no matter what."

Matt heard the pride in his father's voice, clearer than the words he spoke.

Mr. Tyson started the van. "Can we go home now?" Matt asked.

His father looked at him. "I think maybe we'd better go up to the hospital and have your wrist looked at first."

It was badly sprained, not broken. The doctor splinted and taped it, and told Matt to wear a sling for a week. "Can I play football then?" Matt asked.

He could see his father shaking his head.

"Not that fast, I'm afraid," the doctor said. Matt knew it wouldn't matter anyway. Not this year.

As they walked back to the van, he wondered if the team had won the game that day. He wondered for the fiftieth time if Allie was okay. "Did Allie call?" he asked.

"She and her father are back at the house, waiting for us. She's fine—a little scared still, maybe, and worried about you. They came by to thank you for rescuing her."

"Aren't you still mad at him, Dad?"

"No, not really. We'll never see eye to eye about things like this—and he was pretty mad at me for letting you stay in jail. . . ."

"That's not fair. I said I'd take the consequences."

"Right, Matt. And you did. For long enough. You're okay, kid." His father stopped walking, and reached out and pulled Matt toward him in a gentle hug.

Matt put his head against his father's shoulder and brushed away the tears that he couldn't stop. His father wasn't angry anymore. And Matt could trust him again. There wasn't anything better.

AS they drove up, Matt saw all the lights on in their house. The door opened, and everybody came out on the porch. Matt could see Paul was there, holding up a sign that said HANCOCK 49, HIGHLAND FALLS 7.

They're all waiting for me, he thought, and I don't know what to say. The night was clear and starry, and the air felt very cold. Matt shivered.

His father took off his own jacket and gently put it around Matt as they walked to the house together.

"We won, Matt," Paul yelled as they got to the steps. He put up his hand for high fives. He was careful, looking at Matt's other arm in its sling.

Mrs. Tyson put her arm around Matt's shoulder and led him toward the door. Allie was smiling at him, looking as though she had a lot to say but was too shy to say it.

Mr. Behringer said, "Thanks, Matt. That was some tackle!"

Finally, Allie got up her courage. "I think we won, too, Matt," she said.

MARGOT MAREK received a B.A. in English from Swarthmore College and an M.A. from Columbia University. She spent most of her professional life working with learning-disabled and emotionally disturbed children and was an ardent campaigner against all forms of war. Ms. Marek died soon after she finished writing *Matt's Crusade*.

God bless you, Margot.
What _else_ did you write?
2011

Play to win? Gary just wants to walk again.

WINNING
By Robin F. Brancato

A week ago he was "superjock" senior Gary Madden, hero of the high school football team with prospects as limitless as his own imagination. Now he lies in a hospital bed, the victim of a freak accident that's left him completely paralyzed. Overwhelmed by the flood of good wishes and kind advice from friends and family, one question continues to haunt him. Is life as "superquad," the all-star patient, really worth it?

An ALA Best Book for Young Adults
A Library of Congress Children's Book of the Year

A BORZOI SPRINTER PUBLISHED BY ALFRED A. KNOPF, INC.

She risked her very life to solve the
mystery of her father's death, only to find...

THE RUBY
IN THE SMOKE

A mystery by
Philip Pullman

"Beware the seven blessings..." When she utters these
words, sixteen-year-old Sally Lockhart doesn't know their
meaning. Yet when an employee of her late father hears
them, he dies of fear. And thus begins Sally's terrifying
journey into the seamy underworld of Victorian London,
in search of clues that will solve the puzzle of her father's
death. Pursued by villains and cutthroats at every turn, she
at last uncovers two dark mysteries. One involves the
opium trade; the other, a stolen ruby of immense value.
Sally soon learns that she is the key to both—and that it's
worth her very life to find out why.

Winner of the International
Reading Association's Children's Book Award —3
An ALA Best Book for Young Adults

A BORZOI SPRINTER PUBLISHED BY ALFRED A. KNOPF, INC.